Jake for Mayor

To Christine,
    Hope you like Jake.

        Joy Aguilar

To Christine,
Hope you like it.
[signature]

Jake for Mayor

by

Lou Aguilar

www.penmorepress.com

Jake for Mayor by Lou Aguilar
Copyright © 2016 Lou Aguilar

ISBN-13: 978-1-942756-02-6(Paperback)
ISBN :-978-1-942756-03-3 (e-book)

BISAC Subject Headings:
FIC016000   FICTION / Humorous / General
FIC052000   FICTION / Satire
FIC027270   FICTION / Romance / Clean & Wholesome

Editing: Chris Wozney
Cover Illustration by Christine Horner

Address all correspondence to:

Penmore Press LLC
920 N Javelina Pl
Tucson AZ 85748

Reviews

"Lou Aguilar has crafted an original, American story—perhaps the first ever about a literal and figurative political underdog—and the results are, under former DC journalist Aguilar's pen, knowingly topical, briskly plotted, and hilarious. You'll wish Jake was your mayor."
—J. Ryan Stradal, author of *Kitchens of the Great Midwest*, 2016 *New York Times* Bestseller in Fiction.

"Veteran screenwriter and former Washington reporter Lou Aguilar has produced a novel that draws on all his talents. In *Jake for Mayor* he tells the (slightly true) story of a political campaign gone wild, with the most improbable candidate ever, a mischievous dog. It's a tale that will appeal to readers of all ages—and may strike political players as much too close to home."
—Michael Barone, *Washington Examiner* senior political analyst and co-author of *The Almanac of American Politics*.

"*Jake for Mayor* is a hound for all seasons—part drama, part comedy, part election satire and all funny. Young readers will fall in love with the titular canine candidate, and their parents will be hooked by the political farce and the Capra-esque love story. A deftly written, completely satisfying modern fable."
—Bryan Curb, Emmy-winning director and Executive Producer of *Lucky Dog* on CBS.

Dedication

To my dad, Lundy, noted scholar, revered teacher, and yet frustrated novelist. In the end, he gave birth to one.

Acknowledgements:

My sincere thanks to Tammy Norton for bringing me the true story, and conceiving the fictional one with me.

Thanks also to Marisa Finotti for guidance through the novelty of novel writing.

And further thanks to Victor Macia for expert technical advice on construction sites.

Part I

DOGGED

Chapter 1

The children were my best props ever. Over eighty of them overran the Lost Dutchman State Park picnic area on a cold sunny morning, the first Saturday in October. Most of the kids fell within the picture-perfect age of twelve to fourteen, with forty percent of them female, which was demographically ideal for my purpose.

Cheerful parents brightened the image. My candidate glad-handed them under a large, twin-pole supported banner that read *53d Annual Patrol Youth Picnic—Sponsor, Congressman Bob Morris*. A smaller banner below heralded *Bob Morris for Arizona Governor—For Our Families and Our Future*. I liked using alliteration to sell a point and, in this case, a politician.

Visually, Bob Morris was an easy sell: forty-nine years old, jovially plump with short brown hair that was starting to grey. Wearing a green wool sweater, he looked like an old TV dad from when TV fathers knew best, before they became cartoonish boobs. Leaving nothing to chance, I had buttressed Morris with two actual television stars: Roscoe the Elephant and Bruce Nelson of Phoenix 5 News.

Roscoe, of course, was not the genuine PBS celebrity but a struggling local actor in a blue two-legged elephant suit, flapping trunk included. His mission was to entertain the younger siblings of the newly minted patrol crew, while the seventh graders engaged in more mature activities, such as inter-gender conversation. If the little kids near the snack tables suspected a fake Roscoe they never let on; his silly speaking-singing voice over a loudspeaker sounded close enough to the original.

Bruce Nelson appeared less involved. The dapper black TV reporter leaned against a thin sycamore tree, his crossed arms barely holding a wand microphone, while his muscular and bald camera man, Joe, shot cover footage of the festivities. Since low energy was not helpful to my campaign, I approached Nelson with my best accusatory face.

Nelson saw me and came alive. He spoke into his headset mike, then signaled to Joe. The camera man set up a shot with Nelson and me in the foreground and Morris in the background, amusing a crowd of parents. I got ready for my close-up, hoping my 32-year old boyish good looks, thick, short-cut brown hair and fit 5'8" frame in blue jeans and white linen shirt would convey youthful enthusiasm for Morris.

Nelson gave the camera lens a smoldering look and spoke into his hand microphone. "Jane, the fifty-first annual Patrol Students' Picnic is a hit of elephantine proportions. And that's great news for its sponsor, State Senator Bob Morris, who's hoping to ride his family values bandwagon right into the Governor's mansion next month. With me is Morris's campaign manager, Ken Miller. Ken, your candidate seems to be picking up steam in the polls. What's behind his recent surge?"

"Bruce, you said the magic word—family. Traditional family values have been ignored by the Marquez Administration. As Governor, Bob Morris will fight for those values, and make family once more the bedrock of Arizona life."

"Looks like he already has one big endorsement, from Roscoe the Elephant."

Joe swiveled the camera lens to the snack tables, where Roscoe was doing a silly dance for his appreciative brood.

Nelson lowered his mike and turned to me. "Well, did I do your little script justice?"

"I wrote it but you sold it," I said. "A deal's a deal."

I stuck out my hand, palming two tickets to the Phoenix Suns game that night. Nelson shook my hand and pocketed the tickets after a quick glance at the top one.

"Hey, you said courtside."

"Best I could do," I said. "After the election, I'll have more clout as the Governor's Chief of Staff. Wink, wink."

"Okay. Tell Morris I'm ready to interview him. Can you get him next to Roscoe?"

"Sure."

I waved to Roscoe the Elephant, who was taking a breather from his act. He excused himself to his little fans and came toward me. The children turned their attention to the breakfast snack tables laden with fruit: bananas, apples, peaches and grapes, plus donuts for the more rebellious youth.

Jake for Mayor

Roscoe and I walked toward Bob Morris as he concluded his "impromptu" speech (written by me) to the swollen crowd of parents: "And together we can send a message to the fat cats in Washington, that our family values are non-negotiable. Thanks for listening to me. God bless you all. And God bless Arizona!"

The parents applauded. Morris waved to them, then joined Roscoe and me.

"Very inspiring, boss," I said.

"Yeah, these conservative parents are like trained seals. Throw 'em some fish and they'll clap for more. How'd it go with Bruce Nelson?"

"I'd say two more points in the polls."

Something in the air had changed, but nothing hit me right away, apart from a dull stomachache.

"Good job, Ken. Can't wait to lose these little brats and go get hammered."

My stomachache turned acidic, still with no explanation.

"Though I wouldn't mind a couple of their moms joining us. Did you see that Latina in the yellow skirt? I could dance a salsa with that hot mama."

I sensed before I knew that disaster had struck. It was in the silence, the absence of even child sounds. I looked around and saw everyone staring at us, kids and parents. Morris also felt the change in mood, and frowned.

"What's going on?" he asked.

I turned to Roscoe, reached over, and lifted his elephant trunk. The crucifix-size throat microphone looked to me as big as a cross—mine. I tapped it twice, and heard two corresponding thumps on the loudspeaker. I had one brief chance to salvage Morris's political life. I addressed the hostile crowd.

"He said 'llama'! Hot llama!" I heard my own voice over the loudspeaker. "We did a rally at the Tucson Zoo yesterday! They had a couple of llamas there! They spit a lot!"

I saw the crowd mood alter—for the worse—and went into Mr. Science mode.

"Of course, boys and girls, llamas only spit when they're hot. Take the Peruvian Hill Llama for instance—"

An apple flew right at my face. I ducked, and it hit Morris in the forehead. More fruit missiles followed, thrown by future All-American pitchers, while their parents watched with pride. I saw Bruce Nelson and camera man Joe rush toward us. They stopped outside the line of fire. Joe began filming Nelson, now fully animated and talking into his wand mike.

"Jane, we're witnessing what may be the fastest mood swing in political history. Five minutes ago Bob Morris had this crowd eating out of his hand. Now they're biting it off!"

"Roscoe, do something!" I said.

Roscoe the Elephant stepped gallantly in front of Morris, waving both paws at the angry crowd. "Hey, kids. Can't we all just get along? Remember..."

He began his goofy dance and sang.

"It's a wild world all around
From the mountains to the ground,
Let me hear that happy sound,
It's a wild world all around!"

Roscoe pawed Morris's shoulder. "Come on, Mr. Morris, sing along with me!

"It's a wild world all around
From the mountains to the ground,
Let me hear that happy sound,
It's a wild world all—"

"Oh shut up!" said Morris.

He shoved Roscoe, who fell hard on his foam-filled elephant back.

A little blonde girl screamed, "He killed Roscoe!"

"Let's get 'im!" cried a plump boy, waving his band of brothers forward.

Half a dozen angry boys rushed us. I skirted them, then watched as they swarmed Morris and toppled my ladder to success.

Chapter 2

I approached my courtyard apartment building in a fog, unsure if it was meteorological or mental. I couldn't recall the ninety-minute drive back to Phoenix. My brain, which had orchestrated the fastest rise of any candidate since Barack Obama only to see him crash and burn like John Edwards, was still on automatic pilot. I had turned off my cellphone after the eighth desperate call from Bob Morris. There was no saving him now; only myself.

As I neared the door to my second-floor apartment, I heard Bruce Nelson's voice coming through it. The door wood muffled his report but the words "Bob Morris" and "campaign shocker" sounded clear enough. I walked in to see Sharon on our pinewood-frame sofa, her firm, shapely legs over our pinewood coffee table, watching our Sony 40-inch HD plasma television. It displayed a sharp picture of two irate young parents at the Patrol Youth Picnic talking into Nelson's wand mike.

I forewent the usual appreciation of my fiancée's beauty—short-styled black hair over a patrician face, sharp blue eyes behind designer glasses, voluptuous yet gym-hard body evident in grey sweat-shorts and my purple Northwestern University T-shirt—to focus on the TV screen, as she was doing.

"Hey, Shar."

Sharon barely glanced at me and nodded at the television. "You did say you'd get major media coverage today."

"We were all ready to vote for Morris," said the mother on screen. *"We thought he understood our concerns as parents."*

"Yeah, like all the 'blame America' crap in our son's history books," said the dad.

"But he was just lying to us."

"Another liar politician."

I had seen enough. "You mind changing the channel?"

"Not at all."

Sharon remotely switched the channel—to another station showing the "children's riot" at the Lost Dutchman State Park. The graphic on screen read *Video courtesy of KCRT.* I groaned.

"Nice to see rival news shows sharing video footage," said Sharon. "Must be a peach of a story."

"Okay, I had a small setback."

"So did the Hindenburg."

Sharon raised the TV volume on an unseen male reporter's voice.

"State Senator Bob Morris withdrew from the Governor's race today amid a nosedive in public support, spurred by his sexist tirade at a kid-friendly event. Morris is blaming today's fiasco on his inexperienced campaign

*manager, Ken Miller, whom he says wrote the offensive line
as a joke."*

"Pinhead," I muttered, slumping down on the sofa beside
Sharon.

Sharon muted the television then turned to me, and not
with desire.

"It'll be okay, Shar," I said. "There's more than three
weeks left till Election Day. With Morris out of the race, the
Green Party candidate has a chance. Martha Dixon. I called
her to offer my services, and poured on the environmental
drivel: less cars, more dolphins, global warming—or is it
global cooling—anyway, climate change. Blah, blah, blah."

Sharon stood up. She walked into the bedroom, leaving
the door open. I went the opposite way to our tiny kitchen
and grabbed a beer from the refrigerator. I retook the sofa,
drinking and sulking.

"Guess we won't be having champagne dinner with the
Morrises like we planned," I said. "So where do you want to
eat tonight?"

Sharon stepped out of the bedroom, wearing a long side-
slit khaki skirt under a pink cashmere sweater and carrying a
full compact blue suitcase, which she put down in front of
me.

"Going somewhere?" I said.

"The airport. I'm flying back to Chicago in two hours."

"What?! You're kidding, right?"

"The only joke was on me," Sharon said, adding in a mock
masculine voice, "Come with me, babe! We're gonna ride the
Morris Express straight to Washington DC!"

"I'm telling you this'll blow over."

"Like a mushroom cloud. You're radioactive, Ken. And I don't want to stop the world and melt with you."

"Come on, Shar, you love me."

"I'd love you more in a pool than a barrel. Look, Ken, you gave it your best shot. It didn't work out. Time for you to forget politics and go back to advertising."

"Politics *is* advertising."

"And you're much better at deceiving people directly than through some puppet candidate."

"Was that a compliment?"

"I spoke to Daddy," said Sharon. "He still hates you for stealing me away, but you were his best Mad Man. He said if you're back in the office by next Thursday you can have your old job back. Otherwise, quote, 'He can kiss my ass.' It's a good offer, Ken. Take it."

"What about, ah, you and me?"

"My door's still open," said Sharon. "If you love me, you'll come back to Chicago. You'll never find a better match for you than me."

"Yeah, we could be soulmates. If we had souls."

"Good luck, Ken."

She walked out the door without a backward glance.

Chapter 3

I drove east on Interstate 70 through the Colorado Rockies in an interminable snowfall. The gray stone towers dwarfing my new (still unpaid) maroon Mustang made me feel even lower than when I'd slunk out of Phoenix at dawn. I entered the final mountain tunnel like a hare going into its hole. Static replaced Billy Joel on the car radio. I shut it off and stared ahead down the slope-roofed highway, looking for daylight. But all I could picture was the tanned, smug face of Malcolm York of York and Associates, Chicago, watching his former golden boy and almost son-in-law crawl back to the firm.

I exited the tunnel onto a pastoral flatland under a cotton-clouded blue sky. The Rocky Mountain range behind me dominated the whole western rim of the valley. To the north, my left, wild grass rippled beneath tall green pines and autumn-orange trees. A wide, rushing crystalline river paralleled the highway on my right, bending south past a large billboard ahead.

The billboard art was comprised of two separate paintings. One showed a little boy and a cute teen girl eagerly leading their chipper parents toward a glowing entrance under the sign, *Welcome to El Dorado.* The other was a side view of what resembled a long gold bar beside a broad stretch of river, but was in fact a massive shopping mall-amusement park hybrid. The ad pitch read *Coming Soon: El Dorado—Where Treasures Meet Pleasures.* Clever slogan, I thought, in my once and future professional opinion. I credited the *Shaw Development Co.—Erie, Colorado,* referenced in smaller print below.

On paint the structure seemed to blend organically with the landscape. Not so the actual construction site. I could see it in the distance right beside the south-veering river: a monstrous exoskeleton of steel beams, grey concrete and planks. That caterpillar would have a long wait to turn butterfly.

I sped past the billboard, checking my gauges. The radio clock read 3:49, the fuel arrow close to empty. I knew I should have filled up before the Rockies. There was no gas sign in sight, only a small road sign indicating *Erie—Next Exit.* I searched for the turnoff and still almost missed it, a narrow down ramp just past the river bend. I took the exit and went way off my course in life.

I merged on a narrow unmarked road, barely wide enough for oncoming traffic, which luckily was nonexistent. The ubiquitous river reappeared on my right, flowing toward the distant mountains. Ranch land surrounded the road, grazed on by serene cattle behind low wood-rail fences.

My cellphone rang in the cup holder, displaying Sharon's lovely face frozen in a coquettish smile. Her voice sounded garbled, perhaps due to mountain blockage. I deciphered what I could, and answered her. "I'm in backwoods

Colorado, 'bout sixty miles south of Boulder. I'll spend the night there. Should be in Chi-town tomorrow night .... What? .... Alright, Shar, I'll say it. I'm an ad man. An ad... Hello?"

A klaxon blast right behind me caused me to nearly drop the phone. It came from a weather-beaten green pickup truck that was closing fast on my rear. I swerved toward the shoulder of the road, and the truck roared past. I saw the driver's profile for just a split second, but it imprinted itself in my brain: a beautiful feminine profile—short brown hair, button nose, pink, full lips pressed tightly together—in a thirty-something package.

I got back on the road where the ranch land gave way to farm land. Disparate fields reflected the contrast between full-time and part-time agriculture. I approached one under-tended farm on my left, marked by overgrown grass, a white two-story farmhouse, a long dirt driveway and the green pickup truck.

It was idling in the driveway, just off the road, to the right of a two-man surveying team on the grass. Both men wore pale corduroys and ski jackets. A lean man, wearing an orange cap, stood behind the tripod-mounted surveying camera, while a ponytailed heavy guy approached the truck. I pulled to a stop on the roadside opposite the driveway, hoping for a second, better look at the striking truck driver.

My voyeurism was soon rewarded. Truck Girl sprang out of the pickup in a pair of tight jeans that hugged her round hips and firm bottom, with denim legs tucked inside her brown cowboy boots. A half-open red cotton shirt over a black tank-top promoted her impressive chest. I was too far away for a clear view of her face, but got a sense of fury on it as she verbally assailed Ponytail. He met the onslaught with what looked like a leer.

Intrigued by the leading lady of this silent movie, I lowered my window and shut off the engine to make it a talkie.

"Take it easy, Jenny!" Ponytail said. "We're mapping out a shortcut to the mall site from the highway!"

"Not through my property, you ain't!"

"It's only your place for three more months."

"Who told you that?!"

"Mayor did! Said the man who finds the shortest route from town to El Dorado will get a huge bonus. Maybe then you'll finally go out with me!"

"Maybe, Ry, if zombies wiped out every other man on Earth, maybe I'd choose you over the Walking Dead! On second thought, I'd let 'em eat me first!"

Ry shook with apparent rage while Jenny turned her back on him and returned to the truck. He yelled after her. "Still the stuck-up prom queen, ain'tcha! Let's just see how proud y' are when you're workin' under me at El Dorado!"

Jenny drove her pickup twenty yards forward and stopped. A moment later, the truck began reversing, on a fast beeline to the tripod.

"Hank, look out!" Ry screamed.

Hank turned toward the onrushing truck bed and dove out of its path with a shriek. The pickup struck down the tripod and ran over the fallen surveying camera. Moving forward again, it surmounted the metal junk pile, then drove on to the farmhouse.

"And I thought Sharon had a temper," I said.

Lou Aguilar

I started my engine and got back on the road to resume my quest for gasoline.

Chapter 4

The country road lengthened with no further sign of Erie, only fields of wild grass on both sides and the river far to the right. I was getting anxious, given my fuel gauge in the red and the vultures circling in the sky. Okay, so they were crows, but I knew there would be buzzards the moment I left my stranded vehicle; I'd seen enough Westerns.

To dampen my imagination, I turned on the radio. A twangy girl singer was bemoaning her "cheatin' man". I switched the dial and heard a twangy man serenading a "cold, cruel vixen". I hit the tuner again and caught a break from the cowboy music: a twangy preacher confirming that Jesus loved me. I changed back to the twangy girl singer.

I glanced up at the windshield and froze. A brown-and-black dog was chasing a flock of frantic chickens across the road and about to become roadkill. I lurched the steering wheel left, much too hard for the power steering, and lost control of my car. The Mustang flew off the road, went into the grass, spun out and flipped over. My world turned upside down.

I fought back the shock while trying to collect my wits. I was suspended by my seatbelt, the car roof now its floor, the passenger window gone, glass shards covering the roof panel.

A beagle-like head appeared at the glassless window. Its oddly noble face and large round brown eyes belied a mangy mongrel frame, clearly male, about twenty pounds, with black spots. He was the chicken-chasing dog I had nearly hit, which would have spared me a lot of trouble.

"You son of a bi—!" I started to say, then caught myself. "Okay, not an insult."

My cellphone rang. It lay on the car roof under shards of window glass, just beyond my constrained arms' length. I strained to reach it with my left hand and caught an edge of the device. Then a glass needle pierced my forefinger, causing me to drop the phone. Sharon's garbled voice came on the line in speaker mode.

"Ken."

"Sharon!" I yelled. "I crashed the car! Call 9-1-1!"

"About the Fleming account. Daddy says he'd like your input on it. It's your chance to get back in his good grace... Hello?"

The line went dead. I didn't want to join it. Preparing to fall on my head, I pressed the release latch on my seatbelt buckle. Nothing happened. I tried to wriggle out of the straps. They held me tight. After a third attempt, I was still hanging like a bat, feeling more lightheaded.

A dog bark jolted me. The mutt sat by the passenger window, tilting his head rightward as if to get a proper look at me. I gripped the seatbelt buckle and again pressed the latch, this time with all my might. There was a click, and I fell head first on the roof-floor. The dog snorted in what may have been amusement.

I pulled the handle on the driver's door. It didn't budge. Two more tries had the same result. I then crawled through broken glass to the open passenger window. The dog retreated a few steps, permitting me to hoist myself out of the car on my back.

I lay in the tall grass, scanning the sky for vultures. It was getting cold fast, and my jeans and Northwestern sweatshirt offered little protection. Something touched my right cheek. I sat up like a shot. The dog sprang back from me.

"You'd better have an owner," I said. "And he'd better have money for car repairs, 'cause I sure don't."

I studied the beagle's bare neck. He had no collar, let alone tag. "Terrific."

I rose to my feet and approached the upside-down Mustang. Through the broken passenger window, I could see my cellphone among the glass shards. I appraised my multiple hand cuts and decided against reentering the car. I patted my right back pocket. At least I still had my wallet.

I surveyed the desolate surroundings, looking for a human domicile. I saw nothing but wild grass and trees that could have been scenic under pleasanter circumstances. No car appeared on the road. I estimated an hour of sunlight remaining, and probably of life. I began walking alongside the road in my original direction, glancing over my shoulder for any helpful vehicle. Soon I noticed I had a traveling companion: the dog, trotting beside me as if on a leash.

"Get away, mongrel. I'm taking a ride for one."

The mutt ignored me and kept cheerily apace. A quarter mile ahead stood a small road sign. I gradually got close enough to read it: *Erie, CO. Population 1,204—and that's plenty.* There was no tangible sign of Erie.

The dog ran off into right field, zipping through the high grass. Good riddance, I thought. I kept to the road until loud yapping distracted me. The dog was some twenty yards to my right, barking excitedly at me. As I stared, he ran around in a circle, stopped, and barked again at me. Apparently he wanted me to follow him into the field.

"That's alright, hell hound. I'll just stay here on Earth."

I heard an engine noise behind me, and turned to see a large cement truck speeding past my upturned car. I waved eagerly but the big truck roared past me, almost blowing me off my feet. I assessed the car-free road, then the setting sun, and shuddered. Again I heard barking. The dog was still in the field, beckoning me to follow. I took a deep breath, and stepped into the field after him.

Chapter 5

I trudged through ankle-high grass, getting colder by the minute. The dog walked merrily in front as on a familiar path. The first man-made structure that I had seen since leaving the road appeared ahead, a rickety wooden 'Little House on the Prairie' shack that could have been Dorothy's if the tornado had dropped it down on Kansas instead of Oz. The hovel had a collapsed front porch, its right end down in the grass.

"Who lives there—the Children of the Corn?"

The dog walked straight to the shack and sat down on the awry porch near the discolored front door. I approached the place somewhat more warily. If this was the dog owner's home, there would be little chance of a car repair check, more of a chainsaw massacre. I stepped past the sitting dog and knocked on the door. After half a minute, I heard rummaging inside. The door flew open and a shotgun barrel stuck out, pointed right at my face. My arms shot up of their own volition.

I recognized the heavy man behind the rifle, mostly by his ponytail, as half of the surveying team on Jenny's farm, the one called Ry. He wore a long-sleeved gray T-shirt and was chewing up the last of a beef jerky stick.

"Who the hell are you?!"

"I'm just looking for a phone!" I said. "Had a serious car accident back there, and ..."

I caught a glimpse of the dog by my feet and threw a Bible Belt Hail Mary.

"... and your dog saved my life! Hallelujah, brother! Led me out of the wilderness like a prophet of old, right to your doorstep. He's a credit to the canine ra—"

"That overgrown rat ain't mine."

"He ain't—isn't? 'Course not. Dumb mutt almost got me killed—chasing chickens on the road like that."

"You say 'chickens'?"

The shotgun came out through the door, followed by Ry. I kept my hands up while backing off the tilted porch to the grass.

"Hey, man, let's just forget I stopped by and I'll be on my way."

Ry stepped past the lying dog and off the porch. He failed to see the mutt get up on four legs and creep up behind him, as if intending to sniff his butt from porch height. The dog appeared to nibble on Ry's rear, provoking no reaction. A moment later I saw a beef jerky between his teeth, expertly picked from Ry's back pocket. I refocused on the shotgun pointing at my chest.

"Git around back," said Ry.

I perp-walked around the right corner of the shack, wondering how many bodies lay in the surrounding field. The dog returned to my side, chewing on the shorter beef stick.

There was no discernible back yard, just more wild grass encroaching the shack. Near it stood a large, oblong, rusted chicken coop, and R2D2 from *Star Wars*. On closer look, R2 was a broad copper vat with a rubber tube jutting from its head and looping back down like an inverted "U". The vat rumbled and shook from an unseen active motor, churning liquid within. The door to the chicken coop swung in the breeze with nary a chicken inside, only yellow feathers all about. Ry howled.

"Mah chickens! He got mah chickens! Ah'm gonna blow that mangy mutt to hell!"

He shifted the shotgun barrel from me to the dog. The animal gulped down the jerky stick like a last meal.

"Enjoy that jerky, mutt. Chickens'll be feeding on *you* next!"

"Wait a minute!" I said, shocking myself. "You can't just shoot 'im!"

"Oh no? Who's gonna stop me?"

Only a lunatic, I thought, a suicidal one at that. Looking at the dog's sad brown eyes, I turned out to be both.

I charged Ry. As he turned his shotgun back toward me, I gave him my best high school varsity tackle. We hit the ground hard and the shotgun discharged. Buckshot struck R2D2, dislodging the tube on its head. Orange fluid spouted from the top hole like a geyser. I rolled away from Ry, over the shotgun that lay between us.

"Mah whiskey!" Ry cried. "You shot mah whiskey!"

23

With surprising speed for a heavy guy, he snatched up the shotgun. He rose to his feet, pointing the weapon at me while backing toward the vat for a better shot. The dog moved several paces away from me, out of the line of fire. So much for gratitude, I thought. I stood up, preferring to die on my feet. Ry pointed the shotgun at my legs.

"This is gonna smart."

Just behind Ry, the whiskey vat exploded, blowing Ry off his feet. He fell face down in front of me, stone cold, legs spread apart. Steaming whiskey ran down the punctured still, forming a puddle in the grass, then a rivulet to Ry's right leg. The puddle caught fire. A mercurial ball of flame rolled along the alcoholic stream, on course to giving Ry a hot right foot.

The dog shot past me to where Ry lay, straight into the space between his legs. He bit into the right pants leg and tugged. As the flame heated Ry's construction boot, he pulled the whole leg out of the whiskey stream. The mini fireball slid past Ry to the end of the stream and burned out.

Awestruck, I approached the dog. "Holy shit! You saved him. You really are a he... donist."

The dog was slipping the last jerky stick out of Ry's back pocket, the true motive for his good deed. On the ground, Ry moaned.

"Oh, oh. Time to go. You're on your own, mutt."

I hurried away from the shack, further into the back field. The dog reappeared beside me, the new jerky stick between his teeth.

"What are you—the Hound of the Baskervilles? Go hound someone else."

The dog kept up with me, finishing his beef.

It had gotten dark and much colder. I resigned myself to a freezing night on the tundra. Then I saw the light, a dull glow coming over a steep hill ahead. I took the rise like Teddy Roosevelt did San Juan Hill, with the dog my fellow Rough Rider. From the hilltop, I looked down on an encouraging sight at the foot of it.

Erie, Colorado was a slip of a village about a mile wide along the river, terminating a half mile north of it. The third street from the waterfront was the commercial strip, lit by small shops and Victorian lampposts. At the middle, north of Main Street, was a concrete square dominated by a large archaic gazebo. Little rustic houses dotted the darker residential streets.

"Civilization," I said. "Well, close enough."

A couple of miles upriver from Erie, I could see the lighted El Dorado site. The exoskeleton of planks and beams made it resemble a caged serpent waiting to devour the town.

I looked at the dog. "So long, mutt. Enjoy the call of the wild."

I started down the hill. The dog joined my descent.

"I hope there's a dog catcher in this town," I said.

Chapter 6

We walked into Erie on the west end of Main Street, between a redbrick schoolhouse and a small whitewood church with a very high bell tower, both establishments dimly lit for the night. Brighter lights shone one block ahead, where a row of cheerful little shops, bars and restaurants began. Heading toward them, we passed our first Erians, a middle-age couple bearing tote bags full of groceries. They looked askance at me. No doubt my torn jeans, lack of coat, and mangy sidekick gave me that classic homeless look frowned on by town and country fashionistas.

I ignored three more pedestrian stares while seeking urgent warmth, in temperature if not hospitality. The Miner's Diner on the left side of Main Street seemed a promising spot: a narrow 1950s-style eatery, or maybe it had actually been built during the Eisenhower Administration. A sign on the door said *No pets allowed.*

"Aw," I said to the dog. "You can't come in. What a shame."

Jake for Mayor

The dog barked in protest. I opened the glass door just wide enough to slip inside without him. Doorbells tinkled at my entrance. The door closed on the barking mutt.

The diner interior continued the fifties' motif. It was deceptively deep, with reddish vinyl booths along the entire left wall. To the right, near the door, was a long Formica counter with ten cushioned stools, also red; eight in front, two on my end, its far end being the access bar. Oil paintings depicting local landscapes decorated the left wall above the booths. I recognized Erie, the nearby Rockies, and the river. A vintage telephone booth stood against the far wall. On the *Happy Days*-style jukebox, a twangy girl singer celebrated her breakup with her cheatin' man.

All the booths were occupied and most of the counter stools, except for the two nearest me on the door end. Beside one of the central booths, a beauteous short-haired thirtyish brunette in a yellow waitress uniform poured coffee for two lumberjack types. Both men watched her shapely backside as she returned to the counter, where a plump, unnaturally red-haired matron, clearly the boss, set down two hamburger plates.

The beautiful waitress looked oddly familiar to me. I studied her to determine why, and maybe feast my eyes, but the dog's reproachful barking, audible through the glass door behind me, broke my concentration. I moved away from the door and onto the vacant stool.

The waitress grabbed both burger plates and took them to the farthest booth, where some kind of toy-town power meeting was in order. The apparent chairman, facing me, was a handsome gray-haired septuagenarian in a blue flannel shirt, next to a voluptuous forty-something blonde in a rose cashmere sweater. The couple sat across from two fiftyish men in dark suits, their backs to me. I could have sworn I'd seen the older man somewhere before, just like the waitress. Maybe I had died in that car crash and this was a ghost town. Maybe I'd seen too many *Twilight Zone* episodes.

The waitress moved behind the counter and I got my best look at her. Her uniform had distracted me. She was Jenny, the Truck Girl, from back on the road. She took in my unsavory appearance with sympathy rather than disdain. I decided against mentioning our earlier close encounter on the road and the common destruction of Ry's property.

"Miss," I said, "my kingdom for a cup of coffee."

"And where might that be? The railroad yard?"

"It was almost Arizona."

"Too hot for me."

"For me too, now."

Jenny filled a cup of coffee and set it in front of me. I took a long sip, admiring my server. Her penetrating green eyes sparkled with bemusement.

"Sweet," I said. "Your coffee."

"Fresh," she said. "The coffee."

"Uhm, call me crazy...."

"First name or last?"

"Mr. Blue Flannel Shirt back there looks familiar. And I know I've never been here in this lifetime."

"That's Mayor Dunbar," Jenny said, in what sounded like a disapproving tone. "Charles Dunbar, the actor? Picture him in a Stetson. He played Big John Harrow in *Empire*."

My brain pinged. "Oh yeah. That nineties TV show. I read about him. He quit Hollywood like a decade ago to become mayor of some hick...."

Jenny's eyes narrowed menacingly.

"Hickory-pined Rocky Mountain hamlet," I said.

"Right," said Jenny. "Three weeks before reelection, he remembers us simple folk and starts eating at this diner. His fancy wife wouldn't be caught dead in here any other time."

"Re-election. It's a done deal?"

"Seeing as no one's running against 'im, he's got a free ride," Jenny said sourly.

"I take it he's not getting your vote."

"Ever feel like you're the one sane person in a nuthouse?"

"And the more you scream, the more you fit in."

"You got it," said Jenny, eying me more favorably, I thought. "What brings you here, Arizona?"

"My Mustang. It's lying upside down by the road outside town, almost with me in it. Who do I talk to about that?"

"Tiny Perkins. He'll rob you but he's a car healer. His number's in the phonebook, in that booth back there."

"Thanks. Ah, how 'bout your number?"

Jenny smiled. "It's in the book too."

"Under...?"

"Jenny."

"Alright, Jenny, be like that. I'll just divine your number." I pressed my thumbs and forefingers to my temples. "It's coming to me now ... Got it. You're a ten."

Jenny made a short laughing sound.

I smiled. "I'll take a cheeseburger."

While Jenny placed the order, I savored my coffee. I realized that the dog had ceased barking and hoped it had found a new victim. I turned around. He sat just beyond the door, staring forlornly at me. I looked ahead at Jenny, a much pleasanter view, until she left the counter for the booths.

The diner's cozy heat was combining with my physical and mental exhaustion to sedate me. Elbows on the counter, chin in my palms, I fell into a semi-sleep. I could hear voices around me as in a dream, most prominently a boy's through the door behind me.

"Hey, Jake! How ya doin'?! Bet you're hungry, huh! Let's see what mom can whip up for us!"

The doorbells tinkled as a wave of cold air swept my back. Neither disturbed my dreamlike state, nor did Jenny's voice, nor subsequently the boy's.

"Hi, Alex. How was school today?"

"Good."

"That's funny. Miss Garcia called this morning to say you weren't *in* school today."

"That's why it was good."

Jenny audibly sighed. "Where'd you go this time?"

"Mason's Peak. Found an eagle's nest up there. Looks fresh made."

"Oh, Alex."

I heard a dog bark, disturbingly close. Just a flashback, I thought.

"When I said bring your friends, I meant the two-legged kind," Jenny said.

"He's hungry."

Jake for Mayor

"You know the rules. No pets allowed."

"Jake's not a pet. He's his own dog."

"What do you say, Rose?" asked Jenny.

"Heck," said a husky female voice. "I'd rather watch Jake eat than some of our regulars."

"Alright," Jenny said. "What'll you guys have?"

"Turkey on white with fries, and a lemo."

"Turkey on wheat. And he gets scraps."

The dog barked, once again disturbingly close to me. I awoke in a slight daze, with nature calling. There was indeed a boy on the stool beside me, a mid-teen with a cute, sharp-eyed face topped by unruly brown hair. He wore an olive-green denim jacket with a white fur collar, blue jeans and, on his feet, rollerblades. A green knapsack lay on the counter in front of him.

The boss lady, Rose, stood behind the counter, facing the service window. Jenny set down a steak dinner before a wool-capped young man on the middle stool. I got up and walked to the men's room, the last door on the right.

I came out of the small, clean bathroom with fresh eyes, and turned right toward the antique phone booth. Just before it, on my left, Mayor Dunbar's dinner meeting was still in session. I could overhear the conversation even from inside the closed booth, while scanning the thin Erie phone book—more of a phone booklet. Dunbar's thespian voice came through the clearest.

"For the life of me, boys, I don't understand your hesitation. El Dorado's a gold mine. Expect a thousand new jobs in shopping alone. Noah, you're gonna need two hotels to accommodate all the tourists. And that money's going right into your bank, Warren."

"We got nothing against growth, Charles. But the price tag.... times are tough."

"We're a small town."

"But not a small-minded town," said Dunbar.

Good retort, I thought. I delayed my phonebook scan and listened to Dunbar. My brain was pinging. I didn't know why.

"Shaw has sunk twelve million dollars into the construction, against your five. We only need to come up with five more. That's chicken feed for you and your friends."

"Well... when do we get to meet Max Shaw in person?"

"Yeah, Charles, those conference calls won't cut it anymore."

"Come on, fellas," said Dunbar. "You know Shaw's a billionaire recluse. Hasn't left his Australian Outback villa in like, eight years. It's only 'cause he's crazy about *Empire* that he returns my calls."

"Thankfully, not collect," said Dunbar's wife, eliciting chuckles from the men.

"Tell you what, Charles. Soon as you're reelected, you can count on my support."

"Provided you are reelected."

Everyone laughed at this absurd joke.

"You never know," Dunbar said. "Someone might decide to challenge me."

"They got three weeks to do it."

Jenny approached Dunbar's booth, coffee pot in hand, rendering service without a smile. The mayor raised his now full coffee cup in a toast. "To El Dorado."

Everyone else raised their cups. "To El Dorado."

"And to the ranchers, farmers and shop folk it's gonna force out," Jenny said.

Frowns replaced smiles at the table.

"No one's forcing 'em *out*, Jenny," Dunbar said. "Only into different lines of work."

"Yeah, service jobs. Kowtowing to a bunch of fat-cat tourists."

"They'll make more money," Dunbar's wife said.

"T'ain't about the money, Lisa. It's about pride in what they do, in what they grow and raise."

"Jenny, Jenny," said Dunbar. "Stop fretting your pretty little head. Your husband's way of life is over, rest in peace."

For a moment, recalling her assault on Ry's tripod, I thought Jenny was going to pour the coffee on Dunbar's head. But she finished refilling all the cups and walked away.

I found Perkins Car Repair in the phonebook and made my first coin call in years. Tiny Perkins had a deep, gruff voice that made him sound the opposite of small. When I mentioned Jenny at the Miner's Diner, he became less gruff. He said he would tow my car and retrieve my belongings. I exited the phone booth, but instead of heading up the aisle, I paused next to Dunbar's table.

"Excuse me," I said. "Aren't you Charles Dunbar, from *Empire*?"

Dunbar appraised me dismissively.

"I used to be on television," he said. "Now I'm Mayor here. You passing through? We got strict vagrancy laws in this town. I oughta know. I signed 'em."

The rest of the booth crowd chuckled.

"I'm not as derelict as I look," I said. "Fact is, I'm in politics myself, behind the scenes."

"Way behind, I hope," said Lisa Dunbar, to more chuckles all around.

I pulled out my wallet and handed Dunbar my business card. He looked dismissively at it.

"Ken Miller. Political consultant. Who was your last client? Bigfoot?"

More chuckles ensued.

"Bob Morris."

"Arizona Morris? He's last week's bad joke."

"He was doing alright till he went off script. My script."

"So what do you want?"

"Just a minute of your time."

Dunbar looked at his watch. "Wait... wait... go."

I went for it. "I overheard your pep talk here and I thought it was brilliant. The way you turned every objection on its head, smooth. For instance, he said 'small town', and you said 'small-minded town'. Perfect. You currently hold elected office. That's political experience. And you're still a popular national figure, thanks to *Empire*. Two other famous actors went on to be Governor of California. One of them got to be President."

"You sure can gab, boy, I'll give you that. Fifteen seconds."

"There'll be an open Colorado Senate seat next year. With a little expert coaching, you could be the right man to fill it."

"Coaching—from you... as my campaign manager?"

"Yes."

Dunbar leaned back in his seat. "What do you think, guys? Should I throw my hat in the Senate race?"

"You'd disappoint a lot of people."

"We need you here, Charles."

"You heard my constituents, son," said Dunbar. "But tell you what. If I ever need the vagrant vote, I'll give you a holler. You got twenty-four hours to get a job or get out of town." He crumpled up my card.

I looked at Dunbar. Jenny was right. Erie had a creep for a mayor. But it was none of my business. My political career was deader than Elvis. I walked back to the counter, lamenting my fall from grace, and saw I still had further to drop. The dog sat on my stool next to the boy, Alex, munching down French fries in a bowl.

"You have got to be kidding me!"

Alex turned to me, as did everyone else at the counter, other than the dog, who just kept on eating French fries. A concerned Jenny came over from the far end of the counter.

"What's the matter with you?"

"I'll tell you what! That mutt wrecks my car and, when that doesn't kill me, he nearly gets me shot, then blown up, and now takes my seat and my fries! I bet you gave *him* your phone number!"

"His name's Jake," said the boy.

"Jake! Jake is it! Well, Jake, one of us isn't welcome here! And I think it's me!"

I turned to leave. The dog appeared ready to go with me.

"No, don't get up," I said. "As long as you're sitting there, nothing more can happen to me."

I started for the door. It swung open in front of me. A tall, square-jawed, fiftyish man in a white Stetson and a brown corduroy jacket blocked my exit, with little need of the holstered pistol on his right hip.

"Ken Miller?"

I gulped. "Yes?"

"You're under arrest."

"Arrest?! Me?! What for?!"

"Assault and arson."

"What?!"

"Hands behind your back."

"Wait!" I said. "It wasn't me! It was him!"

I pointed at the dog on my counter stool. Everyone around me turned to him. Jake seemed to feel the multitude of eyes upon him and looked up from my fries, sheepishly nibbling the one already in his mouth.

"What's going on, Toby?" Jenny asked.

"Ry Coogan said this fella jumped him and blew up his house."

"The dog did it!" I said. "Ask him about the chickens! Go on, ask him!"

"We may have a live one here," Sheriff Toby said to Jenny almost under his breath.

"I'm innocent I tell you! You got the wrong mammal!"

"Toby, wait," Jenny said. "Maybe he's telling the truth."

"The dog blew up Ry's place?"

"Well..." Jenny said uncertainly.

I kept pointing at the dog. "Look at his face! He's got guilt written all over it!"

"Tell you what, son," Sheriff Toby said. "You come along quiet-like, and I'll take the dog in, too."

I turned to Jake. "Ha! Thought you'd get away with it, didn't you! You're going down with me!"

"Uhm, I don't have any paw cuffs," Toby said.

"I'll bring 'im in, Toby," Alex said, standing up. "Get down, Jake."

Jake jumped off the stool to the floor. Sheriff Toby sighed and bent over the dog.

"You, ah, got the right to remain silent. If you waive that right, anything you say can be used against you in a court of law."

"I've heard of animal rights, but this is ridiculous," I said.

"Your turn," said Sheriff Toby, handcuffing my wrists behind my back.

Chapter 7

My jail cell was a grey concrete cube, twelve feet by ten, with a front barrier of black mesh that camouflaged the sliding cell door. Mid center on the back wall was a barely openable window with outside bars, the windowsill at nose level. A knee-high slab extended from the right wall to double as bench and bed. The exposed steel toilet and sink furnished the left wall. In front of the cell a tight, short corridor separated it from the tiny sheriff's station that I had come through. The hallway door was shut.

I knew the exact diameter of the prison since I'd been pacing around in it for the nearly two hours since Sheriff Toby Harris had incarcerated me with the dog. Jake sat on the floor under the window, next to a tin cup of water, watching me pace and hearing me rant.

"There I was, halfway to Chicago, a six-figure salary awaiting me, and I run into you!"

Jake barked once, as if in protest.

"Okay, so it's in advertising. Beats the heck out of this place. Boy, did Sharon let me have it. I use my one phone call on her, and she blames me for this mess. Said she'll ask her daddy to hold the job till next week. Fat chance. With good behavior, we'll be out of here in a year."

Jake barked.

"I know that it's seven in dog years. That's your problem."

I heard the cell door slide open. A hatless, coatless Sheriff Harris entered my cell, revealing his buzz-cut brown hair and white uniform shirt with badge. He was holding a small picnic basket laden with breadsticks and chicken thighs.

"All right, supper," I said. "Thanks to you, I didn't get to eat at that diner. Say, that's some fancy jail food."

"Yeah," said Sheriff Harris. "One of the town moms whipped this up. I'm sorry, Miller."

"Sorry? For what? Looks delicious."

"It's for Jake."

"What?! For the dog?! You're joking, right?"

" 'Fraid not. Jake's real popular with the kids in town, including the lady's son, Pedro."

"Why that's—speciesism!" I said. "And I'm on the wrong end of it."

"Deputy Smith'll walk Jake when he's done eating."

Harris lay the basket on the floor next to Jake's water cup. Jake bit on a drumstick, devoured the meat and began munching on the bone. I stared hungrily at the rest of his food. Jake seemed to notice this. He bit on another drumstick and brought it over to me, as if offering me the mostly intact treat.

"I don't need your charity," I said, grabbing the drumstick out of Jake's mouth.

I took a bite. It was delicious.

"Did you check out that shack for a moonshine still?" I said.

"Sure did," said Harris. "No trace of one."

"It was there, Sheriff. I swear. It's what caused the fire."

"To tell you the truth, Miller, I believe you. But Ry Coogan works for Shaw Construction. He's foreman of their El Dorado crew. Two of his boys could'a easily hauled off that still. 'Fraid you picked the wrong guy to tangle with."

"Like I had a choice."

"The good news is, Judge Briscoe set your bail. You pay it, you go free for a spell, under two conditions. One, you don't leave town 'til after your trial."

"When's that?"

"Day the judge gets back from vacation, in three weeks."

"Three weeks! Are you kidding me?!"

"He's gone fishing in Saskatchewan."

"Just had to get away from the bustle of Erie," I said. "I've got to be in Chicago next Monday."

"Only as a fugitive."

"What kind of town is this?!"

"My kind of town," Harris said.

I got the song joke. "Well, I'd rather not spend the whole time in jail. How much is my bail?"

"Five thousand."

"Five thou—?!" A chicken bone caught in my throat. I started to choke on it.

"Water!" I gasped. "Need water!"

Jake pawed at his tin cup and barked, as if pointing it out to me. I scooped up the cup and chugged all the water. Seeing dog hairs in the cup, I dropped it like a live rat.

"I have six hundred bucks left to my name," I said.

"Credit card?"

"Maxed out paying off Arizona debts."

"Family?"

"We're—estranged."

My father taught English Literature at Ithaca College, which suited his Dickensian attitude. He had given the same speech to my older sister and me before each of us left for our senior year of college. "With this check, I complete my financial obligation as a parent," he said. "Henceforth, all our dealings will be strictly familial." There had been precious few of those since, although much of that was my fault.

"Friends?" Sheriff Harris asked.

"None five grand's worth."

"Hmm," said Harris. "I'll look into some kind of work release for you in town. But there's one other condition on your bail."

"Forty lashes?"

"Judge made you responsible for your cell-ma..."

"Free Jake! Free Jake! Free Jake!"

The chanting was coming through the cell window in adolescent voices, four or five of them.

"Free Jake! Free Jake! Free Jake!"

"'Scuse me," said Harris.

He exited the cell into the main station. I pushed my cell window up a crack to its quarter-way limit then stood on my toes to get an unobstructed outside view. The window overlooked a small lighted parking square. Two vehicles sat in the eight-space row nearest the wall: the black Dodge Journey SUV that had brought me in, marked *Erie Sheriff's Department*, and a Honda Civic belonging to the sole other employee, the clerk-dispatcher-deputy.

Beyond the vehicles, four youngsters in their early teens stood shoulder to shoulder, holding up homemade cardboard signs. Each sign had a close-up photo of Jake's beagle face, only behind hand-drawn grey bars. Black letters over two of the pictures declared "Free Jake!", with "Jake no rake!" above the other two. Alex from the diner and a lovely, well-developing brunette with shoulder-length hair occupied the center, flanked by a Hispanic boy and a black boy. The youth quartet resumed chanting.

"Free Jake! Free Jake! Free Jake!"

"It's Dog Day Afternoon," I said to my cellmate.

Curious passersby kept approaching the kids from both side streets. The youths would talk to them, point to my cell window then hand them "Free Jake!" flyers with the same doctored dog picture as the signs. Sheriff Harris appeared before the youngsters, once more in his cowboy hat and coat.

"Alex Garret, does your mom know you're out here?"

"She's supporting us," said Alex. "We're protesting the jailing of Jake the dog."

Brunette Girl looked admiringly at Alex, who was obviously the leader of the pack.

"It's cool and unusual," said Black Kid.

Brunette Girl slapped her forehead; I pegged her as the brains of the outfit.

"You got 'im cooped up like an animal," said Latino Boy.

"I resent that remark," I said.

"The dog's living it up in there," said Harris. "Beats his normal vagabond state."

He took a closer look at Brunette Girl's sign. "Annie? 'Jake no rake'?"

"It means a dissolute character," Annie said.

"Ah... What's 'dissolute' mean?"

"Prone to vice," I said to the dog. "That's you, jerky thief."

Alex raised his sign. "Free Jake!"

His three comrades joined in. "Free Jake! Free Jake! Free Jake!"

Headlight beams brightened the parking lot and a silver van followed them in, the right side heralding *KTRS Headline News—Boulder.* The van pulled into the closest space to become the third vehicle on the lot. Sheriff Harris and the kids watched the van like it was an alien space pod, as did I.

A gorgeous blonde in her early thirties stepped out the passenger door. She wore a short navy blue skirt with a grey leather buttoned jacket that curved over her chest. Blondie circled behind the van to Sheriff Harris and showed him what looked like a press badge. They had a brief exchange, too low for me to hear, that ended with Harris nodding.

Blondie walked to the van driver's window and spoke into it. A lanky young black man stepped out, wielding a topflight video camera. Blondie pointed to the four young protesters.

"Get those kids in action," she said.

The camera man obligingly pointed his instrument at the youngsters. They began to talk among themselves, obviously grasping the concept of press coverage. Soon they resumed their chanting and sign-waving. Sheriff Harris escorted Blondie toward the station entrance.

"Free Jake! Free Jake! Free Jake!"

I heard Jake bark, then Sheriff Harris's voice over the sliding cell door behind me.

"You got a visitor, Miller."

I turned around and got an eyeful of Blondie's lovely face and figure as she walked into the cell. Her jacket opened on a burgundy silk blouse that displayed prominent cleavage.

"You sure beat a last meal," I said.

"You're Ken Miller alright," said Blondie. "Last seen in Phoenix, Arizona, running the Bob Morris campaign... into the ground."

"Hey, talk about media bias."

Sheriff Harris shut the cell door behind Blondie and left us alone. Jake sat behind the picnic basket, chewing on a breadstick.

"I'm Nina Wallace, *Headline News*."

"You look more like headlight news."

"We're number one in Boulder."

"By staying on top of those fast-breaking ski reports."

"Ha," said Nina. "Bruce Nelson said you were funny."

"You talk to Bruce?"

"More like flattered him. His story on the Morris meltdown has become required viewing for us hungry TV types."

"I'm sorry that I was part of it."

"So's Nelson. He said you got hosed."

"He should know. He was the fireman. You come to drench me too?"

"Just the opposite. You could be my ticket out of Boulder."

"I get it. You're in local news limbo, looking to rise to network news heaven."

"I have the talent."

"Better yet, you got the looks."

"True. But I still need a breakout story."

"You and me both," I said, indicating my surroundings.

"Your name came up during our police scans. It seemed odd to me. A week ago, two Arizona polls had Morris over the incumbent, Joe Marquez, a rising Democratic star, and in the mix for President. I know you did opposition research on Marquez. And now you're in jail in Backwater, USA, charged with arson and assault? My guess is—someone wants you out of the way."

I stared at Nina in surprise. She moved her naturally seductive face closer to mine.

"Come on, Ken. You can tell me. It's a conspiracy, isn't it?"

My brain computer pinged on "conspiracy", telling me just how to act next. I'd seen enough *X-Files* episodes. I became outwardly tense, jittery, and saw Jake staring at me with a puzzled expression.

"You can't report that," I said. "They'll come after me."

"I knew it!" Nina said, looking eager. "Don't be scared, Ken. I'll stand by you. So will my station."

"I—I'm a sitting duck in here. I'll talk, but only in a public place, where I'll be safe. You've got to get me out of here first!"

"How?"

"Pay my bail."

"How much is it?"

"Seven thousand." I needed the extra two thousand to live on.

Nina frowned. "That's a lot of money."

"I know. It's all part of their plan."

"My News Director will yell. But... if I can guarantee him that the story's worth it.... Give me a hint. How high does it go?"

I looked around as if the walls had ears. "All the way to the Whi... no... it's too big. I'll be putting you in danger. Let it go, Nina. Save yourself. Leave me here."

"Wait, Ken," Nina said excitedly. "I'll talk to my N.D. I'm pretty sure he'll pay your bail. We can courier you a bank check tonight. Let's meet tomorrow morning. Where and when?"

"Miner's Diner at ten."

"I'll be there," said Nina. "You won't regret trusting me, Ken. Sheriff Harris!"

The sheriff reappeared to let Nina out of my cell. She hurried to the main station. Harris slid the cell door shut in front of me.

"You can leave it open, Sheriff. I'm making bail."

"Good."

"So... what was that second condition your Hanging Judge put on me?"

"Oh yeah. From now till your trial, you can't let that dog out of your sight."

I deflated. "Oh, come on!"

Jake barked happily.

Chapter 8

Midnight found me walking by the river on a dirt footpath that ran behind the more upscale riverside homes of Erie. Silent lightning speared the barren land across the water. Jake dashed in and out of the shadows, keeping up with me. Twice he skirted the river's edge without falling in. Just as well, since I was legally obliged to jump in after him.

As Nina Wallace had promised, a seven-thousand-dollar money order in my name had arrived by courier at the sheriff's station an hour prior. My concern that some *Headline News* bean counter would check the actual bail amount against the payout sum had proved unwarranted. So once I paid my bail with cash in the morning, I would have two thousand dollars extra for my little Erie vacation. Of course I still needed to concoct a plausible story that would avert a lawsuit against me by KTRS.

Sheriff Harris could have kept me locked up overnight but had decided to trust me, for a better reason than my honor. We both knew I wouldn't get far with him on my trail. I'd seen enough chain gang movies. At his suggestion, I was headed for the Erie Hotel on a dog-friendlier route than Main Street, with my very own ball and chain, Jake.

Far across the river flickered widespread points of light that had to be ranch and farm homes. With each lightning flash you could discern the surreal valley and the Rocky Mountain peaks beyond. I recalled my earlier odyssey through that very wilderness. I'd barely made it out alive. What must have it been like, I thought, to cross this land 150 years ago, braving natural and human perils, never knowing which lurked around each bend. The pioneer spirit had built a hardy nation in record time, so that my generation could be so infantile.

The Erie Hotel compound took up an entire riverside block. This included the handsome six-story brownstone manor in front, the fenced-in garden, the pools and tennis court in back. Jake and I reached the western fence, then turned left up the street toward the hotel's front entrance.

The hotel lobby had pinewood walls and Navajo-style carpeting. Near the right wall, just before the back elevators, was a clubby sitting area with tan leather chairs around an old stone fireplace. Behind the reception desk opposite stood a preppie clerk in a red sweater vest.

"Welcome to the Erie Hotel, Mr. Miller."

"Lucky guess?"

"I was told about your, uh, roommate."

"Sounds better than cellmate."

"Sheriff Harris said to expect you both. Tiny Perkins delivered your luggage about an hour ago. I put everything in your room, five-sixteen."

"Thanks, Peter," I said, reading his name tag.

I charged a week's stay on my debit card for under four hundred dollars and was given a yellow keycard. I rode the elevator with Jake to the fifth floor.

Room 516 was a cozy single with pale blue walls, white carpet, big-screen TV, mini-bar and a large, inviting bed. My two suitcases stood before the long wooden dresser, one with my black wool overcoat draped over it. My cellphone lay on the bedside night table.

"This sure beats our last joint," I said.

The dog flew past me and sprang on top of the bed. He spread himself face down across the bedspread beside the row of pillows.

"Think again, mutt. I've got to share the room with you, not your fleas."

I picked up Jake and carried him into the bathroom.

The shower was a modern water closet with a transparent plastic screen door and a detachable hose showerhead. I put Jake on the tile floor and shut the door on him. He banged his front paws against the screen like a convict in the gas chamber. I got out of my dirty clothes and into the shower with him, then let him have it with the hot power spray. Jake howled as the filth washed off his fur, and whined when I shampooed it. He kept on whining while I took my own restorative shower. I dried myself off with one towel and Jake with the other, him growling the whole time. He leapt out of the stall before I finished opening the door.

I came out of the bathroom to see Jake rolling vigorously on the bed, drying himself further. I grabbed him and put him down on the carpet beside the bed. He barked in protest but lay down where I left him.

I plucked a black t-shirt and underwear from one of the suitcases. Thus clothed, I turned around, looking forward to a well-deserved drink. Jake lay on the bed, face down, legs spread. I stood over him and pointed to the carpet.

"Floor."

Jake reluctantly jumped down from the bed, retaking his spot on the floor.

I took a tiny Scotch bottle from the mini-bar and went over to the curtained window to drink it. First, I slid open the curtain. The magnificent view showcased a lightning storm over the river valley. I sipped the Scotch, appreciating my warm, dry state. I tried to devise a feasible tale to tell Nina Wallace but was much too exhausted. I turned to the bed, ready for the best sleep of my life, and sighed. Jake lay on the bed in his favorite position.

"Floor."

Jake reluctantly jumped from the bed. I lay down in it, and glanced at the forlorn-looking dog.

"Good night, pooch."

I turned off the lamp, and fell asleep in no time.

A thunderclap awoke me. It was pitch black. I heard rolling thunder and heavy rainfall, then crying close to me. No, not crying, whimpering. I turned on the bedside lamp and soon found the source of the lament. On the carpet, Jake was trembling uncontrollably. The louder the thunder, the more he whimpered. I felt something akin to pity.

I scooped up Jake and put him at the foot of the bed. I lay back down. The dog moved closer to me and pressed his head against my hip. The thunderstorm grew louder but his trembling decreased. Jake closed his eyes and went to sleep, and then so did I.

Chapter 9

Sharon licking my ear awoke me. I knew what she wanted, the randy minx. A little predawn action.

"Later, babe," I mumbled, and turned away from her.

That's how exhausted I was. But Sharon wouldn't be denied, and began scratching the back of my neck. I opened my heavy eyes. It was still dark. I flicked on the lamp and turned to my bedside companion. Instead of Sharon's sensuous face, a beagle-like mug confronted me. Talk about a mood killer. I yelped. Jake whimpered.

"What's the matter with you?"

Jake ran around in a circle at the foot of the bed, stopped and whined some more. I looked at my cellphone screen.

"Are you nuts?! It's six in the morning, and storming out there! Use the shower."

Jake barked once more then resumed whining.

I groaned, and got out of bed. I put on my grey sweatpants and Northwestern sweat shirt and shuffled to the door. Jake ran out the moment I opened it. He awaited me in front of the elevator door. When it slid open on the lobby,

Jake flew out, and stopped at the front door like an English Pointer dog.

"Mr. Miller," said Peter, still on duty.

I approached the reception desk, frustrating Jake. Peter produced a pair of plastic poop-scoop gloves and laid them on the desk.

"I won't need those," I said.

"It's a new law."

"Well I'm a new lawbreaker."

"Sheriff Harris told me to insist."

"Talk about the long arm of the law."

I took the gloves, and went out with Jake.

Dawn was breaking on a chilly day with frost on the lawn strips by the sidewalk. We headed toward Main Street. Jake didn't move too far before firing a long spray under a bush.

"Maybe getting up at dawn was a smart move. More time to think up a story for that Megyn Kelly wannabe."

A few yards short of Main Street, Jake paused to poop. I looked ahead at a vintage steel lamppost and noticed a "Free Jake" flyer taped to it. You had to give those kids an "A" for effort. The photo of Jake behind bars looked rather cute. Alex must have taken it on his cellphone camera when he brought Jake to the sheriff's station. Absent the added jail bars, the picture resembled a political ad. My brain pinged at this, but I let it pass. I looked down at Jake's droppings, and donned one of the plastic gloves.

"I knew you were full of crap, just like the last politician I mana...."

The last word stuck in my throat, with my brain pinging like mad. "Managed."

I collected Jake's poop while studying the flyer on the lamppost. Sunlight struck my face like a revelation. I grinned at Jake. He appeared uneasy, probably wondering what he'd done wrong this time.

"You know, you might be good for something after all."

I used the return walk to work out an idea. It was either the stroke of genius or a touch of madness. Which one depended on my breakfast meeting with Nina Wallace in four hours.

An hour later I was pacing around my hotel room while ringing Greg Foster in Washington DC, two hours ahead. Jake lay on the bed asleep. Greg came on the line.

"Ken Miller, you're alive."

"Let's just say undead."

"Hey, what the hell happened in Arizona? Your man was up in the polls."

"He had a hot mic and a big mouth. Bad combo."

"You still in Phoenix?"

"No, in hiding—in a small town you never heard of. Say, how's your Senator doing?"

"A lot better than your guy. He's up a few points. Hey, Ken, if you're looking for work, we're kind of overstaffed right—"

"Don't sweat it, dude. I know where I stand now: the pits."

"I'm sorry."

"Don't be. I may have something going that'll beam me up."

"Hope it's the Starship *Enterprise*."

"Even more fantastic. Tell me, Greg. What would I be worth to your boss if I got a dog elected Mayor here?"

"You mean like Nancy Pelosi?"

"No. Woof woof."

"Are you on drugs?"

"No. But I think I can pull this off, with a little help from local media."

"You get a dog elected Mayor, even in some backwoods burg, you'll be hailed as a genius. 'Course the town itself would be a laughingstock."

"I'll be laughing too, all the way to DC."

"Senator Garrison would be very impressed."

"Great. I'll call you back if my gravy train starts rolling. So long, Greg."

I hung up, and gazed at my golden goose—no, dog.

Chapter 10

The *Headline News* van was parked in front of the Miner's Diner when Jake and I approached it. I wore a green silk shirt and blue jeans under my cashmere coat, which I hoped would make me telegenic. Nina Wallace was nervously pacing near the van, her young black camera man leaning against it. She relaxed when she saw us, then rushed toward me like a lover.

"Ken, thank God. I thought something might've happened to you."

"I'm all right."

"This is Bill, my camera man."

I shook hands with Bill, and the four of us went into the diner.

The place was full of customers but had one vacant booth near the counter (reserved by Nina). Jenny flitted expertly between the booths and counter, while Rose oversaw all other operations. Jake and I took one side of the empty booth, across from Nina and Bill. Jenny appeared before us, smiling at my new non-homeless appearance.

"Three coffees please, Jenny," I said.

Jake barked once.

"And a water."

Jenny withdrew.

"As expected, my ND threw a fit over the seven grand," said Nina. "He only approved it when I told him how earthshaking your story will be, and how brave you're being." She reached across the table and put her hand on top of mine. "You have nothing to be afraid of, Ken."

Jenny reappeared with four coffee cups, one full of water. She noticed Nina's hand over mine and seemed to smirk. Jenny placed the cups in front of us people. Jake began lapping up his water. Bill and I ordered the scrambled eggs with bacon special, Nina a fruit salad, and Jake just bacon (through his spokesman, me). Nina looked expectantly at me. I nodded.

"Bill," said Nina.

Bill began videotaping me, which led some customers to turn in our direction, the closer ones to eavesdrop on my (rehearsed) speech. Jenny stood beside the counter, also listening.

"They say heroes come in all shapes and sizes, but I always thought they had to be human. That is until yesterday, when my world, and car, got turned upside down."

Nina nodded attentively, if with a perplexed frown.

"There I was, stuck in my seatbelt harness, the engine on fire, flames rising all around me, smoke choking me to death!" Okay, so I was exaggerating. If she did any fact-checking at Perkins Car Repair I could find myself in hot water, but I was relying on the inherent laziness of television reporters. "I was done for. Then, up on a hill, I saw *this* gallant creature."

I stroked Jake's head. He gave me a puzzled look.

"He charged down the hill like Rin Tin Tin, straight toward my burning car and burning me."

The noise from surrounding utensils, plates and conversation had ceased, my voice the only sound. Directly across the table from me, Nina's frown increased.

"I still don't know how he got my car door open. Dog stood on his hind legs, pawing at the handle, until I heard a click. He came into the smoking car and chewed right through my seatbelt strap like rawhide. I fell head first on the car roof, just barely conscious. Jake chomped on my shirt and, and straining with effort, he dragged me out to safety."

Nina looked aghast.

"The irony hit me afterward. How a man can be a vicious animal, yet a dog stalwart and noble. We can all learn a lesson from Jake the dog."

I stroked Jake's head. Half the diners burst into applause. Bill moved his camera around to videotape their beaming faces. Nina didn't clap, smile or move. She just sat there seething.

A pretty young mother appeared beside our booth holding a boy of about three in one arm. "Mister, you mind if I take your dog's picture outside with my kid?"

"Why no," I said. "Jake just loves children."

Jake paid the couple no attention while lapping up water. I elbowed him in the side, forcing him off the seat to the floor. Enchanted diner customers began to gather around Jake, petting him. A burly farmer-type lifted him up and carried him outside. Half the diners followed them. Nina and Bill remained, she glaring at me. I nervously eyed the butter knife by her hand.

"I'm ruined!" Nina said. "Seven thousand dollars for a Dog Bites Man story! You tricked me! I'm gonna sue you for ten times that bail amount!"

"You can do that, and look like a sucker. Or you can get what you really want."

"You back in jail?"

"No, Nina. National news stardom."

"What are you talking about?"

"Go with my story. Don't fight the fluff; pour it on. Play up the cutesy factor for all it's worth. Small-town Dog Saves Visitor. Your viewers'll love it. And the sexy yet sincere face reporting it."

"I don't know..." said Nina, looking less hostile, more pensive.

"Trust me. It'll go national." I hummed several bars of a generic network news theme, then imitated the stereotypical announcer. "From New York, this is *Fox News Watch* with Nina Wallace."

Nina's eyes lit up, with something other than anger at me. She turned to her camera man.

"Bill. Get some footage of that dog with those people while I talk to them."

Bill dashed out, wielding his camera, followed by Nina. Jenny appeared with our breakfast order.

"Pretty smooth, Ken. I thought that dog was your worst enemy."

"But he's man's best friend. He could be yours too, Jenny."

"What do you mean?"

"You really like this town, don't you?"

"It might be Paradise, 'cept for the Serpent running it."

"Dunbar."

"That giant tourist trap of his'll be the end of us."

"Why don't more people see that?"

"They been moonstruck by easy money," said Jenny. "Once El Dorado opens its doors, they reckon they'll be sitting pretty."

"But what if Dunbar were to lose the election."

"I told you, no one's running against him."

"Three weeks to go. Someone might."

"Oh yeah, like who?"

I looked straight into Jenny's green eyes. "Jake."

"Jake who?"

I nodded at the glass pane window, through which could be seen a crowd of townspeople celebrating Jake, while being filmed by Bill and interviewed by Nina Wallace.

"The dog?! You laughing at me, boy?!"

"Hear me out, Jenny. 'Jake for Mayor.' He's cute. He's lovable. And..." I gestured at the window, "... you can see how popular he is, thanks to my tale."

"He's a frickin' dog."

"Right. So his campaign will echo what you've been saying. That this town is going to..."

"The dogs," said Jenny. "But a dog can't be mayor."

"Maybe not. But he can make folks think twice about voting for Dunbar. The more votes Jake gets, the worse Dunbar looks, right?"

"It can't work," said Jenny with less conviction.

"But it might make a difference."

Jenny's emerald eyes bored into me, making me want to squirm.

"Why do you care? You don't even live here."

"Maybe I'd hate to see Paradise Lost," I said. "Will you help?"

"What can I do?"

"Come to my hotel room after work."

"Oh?" Jenny said, with a cynical edge to her voice.

"With your son."

"Oh," said Jenny.

Chapter 11

Jenny Garret directed me to the Erie Town Hall, a white-brick, two-story Tudor on the east end and north side of Main Street. At the top of a few wide steps, four marble columns held up the gable, more to draw attention than bear any real weight. The building housed the Mayor's office, a single courtroom, and the judge's chamber, plus two rooms that I had business in: the Permits Office and the Erie Historical Library. I hoped that neither one closed for lunch.

Jake and I reached the Town Hall steps just before noon, just in time to see Mayor Charles Dunbar scurrying down them. He nodded at me without recognition at first, then stopped to stare at me with a scornful expression.

"Well, well," he said. "You look rehabilitated already."

A low growl escaped Jake, directed at Dunbar.

"I took your advice," I said.

"About?"

"Getting a job, to stay here in town."

"Oh yeah? I thought we had enough dishwashers."

Jake growled again, a low but fierce rumble.

"Something more in my line," I said.

"Not much call for a political campaign manager round here."

Jake growled again.

"You never know. There's that mayoral election in twenty days."

"Good luck finding a candidate."

Jake growled.

"I already have."

"Who?"

"You're looking at him."

Dunbar snorted. "You? You're even more delusional than I thought."

Jake growled, and circled behind Dunbar.

"Did I say me?"

"I don't see no one else here."

"That's because he's already nipping at your heels."

Jake chomped on Dunbar's pants leg and began tugging it with dreadful snarls.

"Let go of me, you stupid mutt!"

"Jake!" I said.

Jake released Dunbar's trouser leg. He calmed down, but growled every time Dunbar spoke.

"You're running a *dog* against me? You're mad."

"Rabid," I said.

"It's not even legal."

"I came here to find out. You'll be the next to know."

"I'm warning you, Miller. It's best you leave town."

"And violate my bail? Not me. Face it, Mr. Mayor. You're going to get a real race this time. And in any race, four legs are better than two."

Dunbar scowled, then walked away from me.

Chapter 12

I sat on my bed with my back to the headboard, among five library books, a box from Erie Printers, my laptop, and a dog asleep by my stocking feet. A sixth book, *The Colorado Rivermen*, lay open on my lap, divulging the history of Erie, Colorado. Jake grunted when the laptop sounded an incoming call. I replaced the book on my lap with the computer and clicked on Sharon's pretty face. The live version appeared on my screen, from her luxury apartment living room.

"Hi, Shar."

"Ken, good news. Victor Fleming asked for you personally to handle his beer account. Daddy huffed and puffed but agreed to take you back after your silly trial."

"Will you?"

"My door's still open. For how long depends on you."

"Don't you worry. I'll be out of this ghost town in nineteen days."

There was a knock on my door. Sharon heard it.

"Who's that?"

Lou Aguilar

"Er, must be the maid. Gotta go, babe. Love you."

I closed the laptop on a curious Sharon.

"Come in."

Jenny Garret entered, looking luscious in hip-hugging jeans and breast-hugging red shirt. I stood up, almost in salute.

"Well. Civilian life agrees with you."

"I don't go to bed in a waitress uniform."

"What *do* you go to bed in?"

Jenny smiled, and surveyed the books on my bed.

"Whatcha been doing in here?"

"Launching our campaign. Today I officially registered Jake as a candidate for Mayor."

"No law against a dog doing that?"

"None that I found."

"They must'a thought nobody would be that loco. They didn't count on you."

"That's right. Hey."

Jenny smiled.

"Now, Dunbar knows we're doing this," I said. "I ran into him outside Town Hall."

"Wish I could'a seen his face."

"It wasn't pretty. Would you like a beer?"

"Sure."

I got two bottles out of the mini-refrigerator, twisted one open and handed it to Jenny. She sat down on the bed and petted an appreciative Jake. I opened my beer and clinked bottles with her.

"To Jake for Mayor," I said.

"Jake for Mayor."

"If I'm right about the local vote, support for Dunbar could be fairly soft, like Hillary Clinton's in '08. The key to eroding it will be to rally the farmers and ranchers."

"How do we do that?"

"We need foot soldiers. Where's your kid?"

"I told him to come straight here after school."

"He's a sharp boy. I can use him."

"That'd be wonderful. He goes into a funk sometimes. Ever since his dad died."

"How, ah, did he?"

"Afghanistan. Three years ago."

"I'm sorry." I was, too. "Though, if I may say so, you seem to be pulling his weight with Alex."

Jenny beamed. "Why thank you, Ken."

Her green eyes seemed to reappraise me. There was a knock on the door.

"It's open."

Alex Garret roller-bladed into the room.

"Hi, Mr. Miller. Mom."

"Call me Ken. I take it you prefer roller-blading to skateboarding?"

"I'm on the hockey team. Helps improve my game."

"Grab a chair, kid."

Alex turned the desk chair around and sat down. Jake jumped down from the bed and began pawing Alex's knee.

"Hey, Jake. How's freedom?"

Alex rubbed the dog's head. I handed him a can of cola, which he popped open.

"I was really impressed by your little protest," I said. "The signs, the flyers, the whole rally. Quite effective. You reminded me of me. Tell me, what inspired you?"

"I can't abide cruelty to animals," Alex said. "When I was eight years old, I shot a robin with my BB gun. The way he fell—one wing flapping hard, not understanding what just happened to him—it broke my heart. I been trying to make up for it ever since."

Jenny said, "Tell him your idea."

"He wouldn't be interested."

"Sure I would," I said.

"I want to start up an animal shelter on our farm, for injured and unwanted animals."

"Noble thought. What's stopping you?"

"We're losing the farm, Ken," said Jenny. "The bank won't extend me Tom's loan. So Shaw Development gets it in the New Year. Dunbar'll see to that."

"Not if he's no longer mayor. Alex, how'd you like to work for me the next three weeks?"

"Doing what?"

"To begin with, passing these out."

I opened the printer's box on the bed and took out a flyer I had designed. It featured my cellphone photo of a "determined" Jake under the tall words *Jake for Mayor* and above the slogan *Curb your local government.* I handed the paper to Alex, who read it and smiled.

"I'm in," he said.

"Great. You are now Junior Campaign Manager of the Jake for Mayor Campaign."

Jake for Mayor

Jake sprang up and bit the flyer, snatching it from Alex's hand. He began chewing the paper into shreds.

"Hey!" said Alex. "The dog ate my homework."

Chapter 13

I stood in the bell tower of the Damascus Lutheran Church peering through a pair of binoculars. It was the tallest lookout point in Erie. Over the waist-high stone parapet you could see for miles in all directions: east, past the edge of town where Main Street narrowed to a country road; north, to the prairie and Interstate 70 (my interrupted route to Chicago); west, to the wild grass field I'd almost died in and the Rocky Mountain range beyond it. I was facing south, looking about a half-mile downriver at a wooden former horse-cart bridge (my source: *The Colorado Rivermen*) that crossed the water to the pastureland opposite.

Jake lay on the tower floor against the western wall, sheltered from a bitter cold afternoon wind despite the sunny blue sky. My warmth came from the thermos of sweet brown coffee and two ham-and-egg muffins Jenny Garret had prepared for me. She'd also suggested this observation spot, and gotten Reverend Michael Sloane's permission. It seemed unremarkable, but during my entire six-month charge of the

Bob Morris campaign, my darling fiancée Sharon had done nothing remotely as supportive.

I focused my binoculars on the horse bridge and the three boys bicycling away on it: Alex Garret, flanked by Pedro Hernandez and Tommy Norton. All three wore backpacks with Jake's flyer pinned to them. Their trail bikes reached the other shore and continued side by side for some 40 more yards. Then Pedro split left and Tommy right toward separate ranches, while Alex made straight for the wheat farm in between.

I kept my magnified view on Course Alex. In the wheat stalks ahead hung a genuine scarecrow. He had a droopy old hat, outspread arms and twigs for hands. Alex bore fast on the figure while drawing a Jake flyer out of his backpack. He rode straight at the straw man and spiked the flyer on his right twig middle finger. As Alex rode away, the scarecrow appeared to be hawking the flyer for all to see. Well done, kid, I thought.

I turned my binoculars to Pedro. His vacant bike leaned against a high corral fence. Pedro stood on the bottom fencepost waving a flyer at a group of cows. I thought he was goofing off, until I saw the bull. It was a muscular black beast with a white snout and two satanic horns. The beast approached the fluttering white paper and the puny boy waving it. Pedro was shouting something at the bull. I lip-read the words, "Toro! Here, Toro!" I gulped. This was not a fair bullfight.

El Toro trotted up to the fence where Pedro stood and looked dully at the boy. Pedro spiked the flyer on the bull's left horn and sprang back off the fencepost. The bull didn't charge. Pedro remounted his bike and rode leftward along

71

the fence toward the ranch house. El Toro rejoined his bovine groupies with the flyer affixed to one horn.

I was about to search out the third musketeer, Tommy, when my binoculars caught a white blur advancing from behind some dark cattle. I focused the image on a splendid white horse with a cowboy on its back. He wore a narrow grey Stetson. In sharper view, Cowboy was an old man with a lined, strong face and longish white hair loose in back, yet he sat ramrod-straight in the saddle like a rodeo star. (I'd organized a rodeo rally in Tucson for the Morris campaign).

Cowboy approached the bull, doubtless intrigued by the fluttering paper on his horn. When he cleared a trio of cows, I saw he had a lower-to-the-ground companion. A splendid collie with gold and white fur paced alongside the horse.

"I didn't know Lassie lived here," I said to Jake. "I would've made her the candidate instead of you."

The collie stayed with horse and rider all the way to the bull's side. Cowboy leaned over the bull's head, plucked the paper off his horn and read it. I had added a notice to this stack of flyers: *Jake for Mayor Rally. 10 AM Saturday, October 17. Meet Jake the Hero Dog.* A smile deepened the lines on Cowboy's face. He put the flyer in his jacket pocket and rode away from the bull, the collie at his side.

I moved the binoculars in search of Tommy. So far my Jake for Mayor Campaign Youth were earning their pay—free cheeseburgers at the Miners' Diner.

Chapter 14

I could hardly believe the crowd size in Town Square. A full hour before the rally start time, over three hundred people of all ages occupied the pavement block park on the north side of Main Street in central Erie. They'd come on a cold grey Saturday morning to see Jake the Hero Dog. Sans Jake, nobody recognized me as I mingled with the crowd in jeans and navy blue crewneck wool sweater.

The square's main stage was a vintage octagonal gazebo with a redbrick base and a whitewood platform accessible via a narrow front staircase. Eight faux marble columns held up the white beadboard ceiling and gray cedar-shingled rooftop. On each alternate eave hung a white cloth banner with "Jake for Mayor" written in bold black paint (artwork by Annie Ross, girl Jake Campaign Youth).

A standing microphone was already on the platform. Behind it stood the Dukes of Hazard; really the Donner Brothers, John and Nick, playing a haunting instrumental version of "Ghost Riders in the Sky" on their electric guitars. The handsome 20-something siblings appeared ready for Nashville, one sporting a small black cowboy hat, the other a mane of blonde hair. The brothers and Jenny made gospel music every Sunday in the single service at Damascus Church. They weren't enough for me. I needed a heavenly choir to pull off this scheme.

I was mixing with the crowd, gauging its upbeat mood, when I spotted the old cowboy rancher from Pedro's bull run. He stood ten yards back from the gazebo, holding a leash on his regal collie, raptly listening to the Donners. A fortyish farmer-type with a sweet looking wife and preteen son greeted Cowboy. I was close enough to overhear them.

"Pretty tune, huh, Sam," Farmer said.

" 'Ghost Riders in the Sky'. My Molly loved it. Played it over and over till the day she... rode on."

"I remember," said Farmer's Wife. "Gave 'er comfort."

"You come to see Jake the dog, Mr. McKenna?" asked the boy.

"Billy," said his mother. "We're remembering Mrs. McKenna."

"S'alright," McKenna said. "Sure did, Billy. Being an old coot, I thought I'd seen it all. But a dog for Mayor, that's a new one on me."

"Can't be any worse than what we got," said Farmer.

"Yeah," Sam said. "Dog beats coyote any day."

The conversation encouraged me. Maybe this mad campaign would be easier than I had thought. Much depended on my Dirty Tricks Team, AKA the Jake for Mayor Youth. It was time to check in on Operation Keep Away. I took out my cellphone and texted Alex. *You in position?* The text came back right away. *Yep. Dunbar still inside. You coming?* I texted back, *On my way.*

Jake for Mayor

I started moving toward Main Street against the still swelling crowd, and ran into Jenny on her way to the gazebo. She looked exquisite in a dark brown velvet jacket that ended at mid-thigh, revealing her long strong, shapely legs, bare all the way down to her cowboy boots. She had to be wearing a miniskirt.

"Jenny, you look amazing."

"I gotta warm up the crowd for you and Jake, don't I?"

"You'll get 'em downright hot with those legs."

"So maybe they'll vote our way."

"I don't know. They're expecting a dog. You're the farthest thing from."

Jenny smiled.

"Where is Jake?" I said.

"With Annie in my truck. You wanted him to make an entrance. Should she bring him out now?"

"No, wait till I get back."

"From where?"

"Dunbar's house. We've got to keep him away from the rally so he won't stop it. Your son has a plan and wants me to approve it. Keep the crowd happy till I get back."

"I'll try."

Along with every other man around, I watched Jenny approach the gazebo. She climbed onto the platform and got behind the microphone, between the Donners. The brothers began a fast, melodic guitar tune. Jenny removed her coat to reveal a black sleeveless T-shirt with Jake's picture on the front, under the words *Jake for Mayor*. Its attention grabbing was lessened by Jenny's legs, fully showcased in a pair of white Hooters-style shorts. If this was her choir outfit, church attendance must be through the roof. The visual treat soon became audial, as Jenny's rich, husky voice came in on the guitar playing.

"When was the last time you got up before the sun,
And watched as the night and day melted into one?
When was the last time you really looked at rain,
Dripping down the gutter, splashing on the window
  pane?
My fondest memories are tied around these things:
Sunday school, bedtime rules, grandma's squeaky
  swing.
Sneaking out behind the barn; my love would meet
  me there.
Tripping in the hallway over grandpa's rocking
  chair.
Back in the country, now I know you're gonna say,
Back in the country, don't you wish that you had
  stayed?
Back in the country where the roses still grow wild.
Back in the country where you walked those
  country miles."

I knew I had something urgent to do, but was transfixed by the Jenny show, as was the crowd.

"When was the last time you saw sundown through
  the trees,
Sitting on the front porch in a cool evenin' breeze?
When was the last time that you heard a bobwhite
  song?
When was the last time? I bet it's been too long."

Jake for Mayor

My cellphone vibrated in my pocket, shaking off my enchantment. I glanced at the text from Alex. *Motion in house. You close?* I hurried off toward Main Street without looking back at Jenny, though her siren song followed me all the way to my car.

"Back in the country, now I know you're gonna say,
Back in the country, don't you wish that you had
stayed.
Back in the country, where the roses still grow wild.
Back in the country, where you walked those
country miles."

I got in my rented Ford Fiesta and sped off toward Mayor Dunbar's house.

Chapter 15

I parked the car well short of Mayor Dunbar's driveway, on a wooded roadside near the river, just east of town. A man-high stone wall guarded the Dunbar acreage, and a black iron gate blocked the long asphalt driveway through it. Beyond the wall stood a small forest of white-barked birch trees. I left the car and pressed my hands against the wall, like someone seeking to stretch his legs after a long drive. Jenny's amplified singing voice could be faintly heard from Town Square, less than a mile away. Seeing no vehicles on either approach, I climbed onto the wall to see over it.

Some forty yards into the birch forest garden, half hidden by trees, was a modern cube-style two-floor mansion of dark brown timber. A gray concrete balcony with a Plexiglas handrail protruded from the master bedroom. I jumped from the stone wall to land gracelessly on the other side. I paused to listen for the roar of an attack dog or the wail of Sheriff Harris' siren. Hearing only Jenny's distant singing, I skulked toward the Dunbar home á la James Bond (Sean Connery persona, of course).

Jake for Mayor

Alex Garret hid behind a birch trunk, four trees back from the house, his cellphone in hand, a yellow skateboard by his sneakered feet. He waved as I joined him. We had a full view of the house, from the main residence to the one-level left wing garage. A front porch made of the same wood as the house extended to the driveway. The driveway terminated in two widening outward curves, left to the garage, right to an outdoor parking nook near the forest edge. Dunbar's Mercedes was alone in the nook, shaded by a low, thick tree branch. On the branch perched a large crow, curiously watching us.

"Any sign of the Mayor?" I said in a whisper.

Alex whispered back. "He came out on the balcony like ten minutes ago, listened to mom's singing for a minute, then went back inside. I guess to find out what is going on."

"He won't like the answer."

"You're right."

"Okay, kid, what've you got?"

Alex whispered into his cellphone. "Alpha Two, show yourself."

"Alpha Two?" I said.

Alex grinned. "We're Alpha Men. You know, like from the video game?"

I shook my head in ignorance. On the garage roof, Tommy Norton stood up into view, his cellphone in one hand, a high-powered water rifle in the other. He raised and waved the rifle like a guerrilla fighter.

"Knock it off," Alex said.

Tommy calmed down.

"What's he doing with that water gun?" I asked.

"Got no water in it," said Alex. "Oatmeal and milk."

I thought about that a moment, and smiled. "Think it'll work?"

Alex shrugged. "It was Annie's idea."

"Annie's a whiz kid, isn't she?"

"She knows a lot."

"And she's super cute."

"I guess so."

"She seems to really like you."

"I like her," said Alex. "She's fun."

"Fun, like Tommy and Pedro."

"Yeah."

"No difference?"

"Well, one big one."

"What?"

"She's smarter than them."

"Ah. Is that all?"

"Good enough for me."

"Maybe not for her."

"Whatcha mean?"

"You'll find out one of these days. And when you do, it may be too—"

The balcony door slid open. Dunbar stepped out, wearing a gold cashmere sweater and holding a portable landline phone to his ear. He looked angry, and soon sounded it.

"A political rally! For a dumb mutt?! Why haven't you stopped it?!... *I'm* the law here, Harris, and I say what's legal or not!... Oh yeah?! We'll see about that! Meet me at the gazebo in five minutes!"

Dunbar withdrew back into the bedroom.

"He's coming out," Alex said. "Get ready, Alpha Two."

Tommy drew back on the garage roof and ducked out of our sight. A minute later, Dunbar burst out the front door, wearing a cream suede coat with a fur collar and designer sunglasses. He strode left across the porch toward the part in the driveway.

"Fire!" said Alex.

A burst of oatmeal shot out from the garage roof and splattered Dunbar's coat and hair.

"What the hell!"

Dunbar halted with a frown. He wiped oatmeal off his coat and inspected it in his hand. He looked up, and saw the crow perched on the tree branch.

"You dirty flying rat! One crow extermination order coming up!"

Dunbar went back into the house. Tommy reappeared on the garage roof. Alex gave him a thumb up. "Get ready for phase two," he said.

I checked my watch. In ten minutes I needed to be back at the rally, to introduce Jake for Mayor. Dunbar had to be kept away from there for fifteen minutes more, a tall order for my Dirty Tricks Squad.

Dunbar reemerged out the front door with wet hair and the same coat, oatmeal free. He moved across the porch toward his Mercedes.

"Fire!" said Alex.

A second oatmeal spray shot out from the garage roof, and splashed Dunbar's coat and head.

"God damn it!" he yelled, glaring up at the crow. "Prophet! Thing of evil! Prophet still if bird or devil!"

He spun around and reentered his house.

"What the heck was that?" said Alex.

"Acting," I said. "I read all about Charles Dunbar online. Before he became a TV star, he was a big-time stage thespian. Guess he's still a ham."

Alex picked up the skateboard and ran with it to the left side of Dunbar's porch. He lay the skateboard on the driveway, snug against the porch edge, pointing at the Mercedes. I checked my watch again. I really had to leave. Alex rejoined me behind the birch tree.

"Worth a shot," I said, deducing his plan.

"Long as he keeps looking up," said Alex.

"Here he comes."

Dunbar came out of his house wearing a green ski jacket and a huge white sombrero. His eyes locked on the crow as he walked the porch toward his Mercedes.

"Come on, Raven, let 'er rip!"

He kept staring up at the crow as he stepped off the porch and onto the skateboard. The skateboard shot forward with Dunbar on it, shrieking all the way. He stayed up a full two seconds before the skateboard shot out from under him, throwing him on his back, the sombrero falling off his head. The skateboard rolled off the parking square into the woods.

"Fire!" said Alex.

A large stream of oatmeal gushed down on Dunbar's face. He wiped some from his eyes, and looked up at the crow.

"Be that word our sign of parting! Get thee back into the tempest, and the night's Plutonian shore!"

"Quoth the Raven, 'Nevermore,' " I said. "Good job, kid. Now for your last trick."

"What's that?"

"Get the hell out of here."

I patted Alex on the shoulder and ran back to the fence.

Chapter 16

I stood on the gazebo platform behind Jenny and the Donners while they did their final upbeat number. The crowd semi-circling the gazebo was about half the town population, more than enough for mob justice if I blew my speech. The trick was to ask them to vote for a dog for Mayor without appearing to insult them as rubes. I was happy to see Nina Wallace among the spectators, interviewing several of them before Bill's camera, until I flashed back to the Arizona state park, and the news-making riot that sank my career.

To calm my nerves, I focused on Jenny's rear, which was every bit as attractive as her front. She finished her song, and the crowd heartily applauded. Jenny waved gratefully, while the Donners packed their guitars and left the gazebo. As she got into her coat, Jenny gave me a radiant smile, which did much to restore my confidence.

"You're a tough act to follow," I said.

"You'll do great, Ken."

"Thanks."

"Everyone'll be minding Jake."

"Thanks," I said, sarcastically this time. "Tell Annie she can bring him in now."

"Right."

Jenny took a phone out of her coat pocket. Alex and Tommy came up to the platform with angelic expressions.

"Men," I said, "You're no longer the Dirty Tricks Squad. You're now Jake's Secret Service. Guard him with your lives."

The boys donned sunglasses and took opposite sides of the platform, where they stood militarily straight. People in front of us parted, making way for the approaching pre-babe Annie Ross, with Jake on a leash, followed by Pedro. Once on the platform, Annie handed Jenny the leash and stood beside Alex, their coat shoulders touching. Pedro joined Tommy on stage right, their coats not touching.

I moved behind the microphone. The crowd stared at me, as did Nina Wallace. Bill the camera man began videotaping me. The Damascus Church bell rang. It tolls for thee, I thought. After the tenth clang, the bell went silent. So did the crowd. I began my speech.

"Hello, everyone. I want to thank you all for coming this morning. My name is Ken Miller."

Out of my left eye, I saw Jake stiffen, fixated on a point deep in the crowd. I followed his look to where Sam the rancher stood, holding a leash. I couldn't see the collie but knew he was at Sam's side.

"I realize I'm a stranger in your lovely town, and that my visit here has been somewhat beleaguered ..."

"Speak English!" shouted a man near the back, prompting a few chuckles.

"Will do," I said, winning back some of the chucklers. "But you don't have to have lived here long to appreciate the attraction of this place, and feel the weight of its heritage."

Jake shot forward, yanking the leash out of Jenny's hand. He bounded off the platform and into the crowd. People danced aside as Jake ran between their feet, moving fast toward Rancher Sam. The leash flew from Sam's hand. I saw the collie making a bee line toward Main Street, with Jake in hot pursuit.

"Go get 'im, Jen!" I said.

Jenny ran forward and leapt agilely from the gazebo to the ground. She dashed through the crowd, which parted to let her through. She followed Jake's route, racing past a fuming Sam toward Main Street. I watched her melt into the crowd, hoping I hadn't lost it as well as my candidate.

"Doggone it," I said into the mike.

Nobody laughed. I cleared my throat. Tough crowd, I thought.

"Your town has a noble history. It was settled a hundred and eighty years ago by brave pioneers, men who fought dirt and dust, rivers and rapids, wild beasts and wild Indians."

Too late, I saw a clearly Native American couple glaring at me from six rows back. I gulped.

"Er, such a man founded this town. His name was Fulton Smith. Smith was a coal miner from another Erie, who came west to work for himself. And what he found here was worth far more than gold... for it was freedom!"

The crowd remained silent, yet more upbeat now. They were mine to lose.

"Charles Dunbar wants to take away that freedom. He wants to turn total strangers into your bosses. That, my friends, is not the Erie way. For when your farms and ranches become one big parking lot for El Dorado, and your fine shops turn into little tourist traps, it'll be too late to do anything about it."

I heard grumbling from the crowd, just the reaction I desired.

"Do you want Max Shaw and a bunch of fat cat tourists bossing you around?"

"No!" came several voices in unison.

"Charles Dunbar does! Shhhhh... listen... do you all hear that?"

Crowd members fell silent as they strained to hear something extraordinary, but they were drawing a blank.

"It's the sound of Fulton Smith turning over in his grave."

Several faces looked wistful. A few nodded.

"You can make a stand like Fulton did. Say 'No' to outsiders, who care nothing for this town! 'No' to more construction! Take what's been built so far of El Dorado for your own local trade. *Your* stores, *your* restaurants, *your* amusements, and yes, your town! Listen to me. Mayor Dunbar is not your master. He's your public servant. And as crazy as it sounds, you can certify that with a single vote nineteen days from today."

There was a more enthusiastic outburst of applause.

"Thank you. Er, at this time I did want to introduce the better candidate for Mayor this election, only he seems to have..."

People stepped aside as Jenny came through from behind them with Jake on his leash.

"Ladies and gentleman, let me introduce the next Mayor of Erie, Colorado, Jake the dog!"

Jake ran up the gazebo steps to eager applause from the crowd. It died out when Mayor Dunbar barged his way through the inner circle to reach the gazebo, accompanied by a morose Sheriff Harris. The two officials climbed the steps to the stage. I stayed behind the microphone.

"Sheriff, shut down this rally now!" Dunbar said.

Jake growled, held back by Jenny.

"On what cause?" said Harris.

"Disturbing the peace!"

"But this is peaceful."

"God dammit, Harris, I'm the Mayor! You do what I say or I'll find a sheriff who will!"

Jake growled again. Sheriff Harris took a deep breath and clenched his right fist. It didn't look good for Dunbar just then. But Harris exhaled through his mouth as if letting out steam. He unclenched his fist and turned to me.

"'Fraid I gotta shut you down, Miller."

"What for?"

"Mayor's orders."

"Is that right," I said, leaning into my microphone head. "You all hear that?! Mayor Dunbar wants to shut us down! What do you say, folks?! Do we let him get away with this?!"

"No!" yelled a bunch of crowd voices.

Dunbar's eyes widened. He hadn't expected such open defiance.

I chanted, "Jake! Jake! Jake!" I turned to Jenny and the five kids on the platform, waving my palms upward. "Jake! Jake! Jake!"

My crew got it, and chimed in.

"Jake! Jake! Jake!"

Jenny waved up her hands at the crowd, and it picked up the chant.

"Jake! Jake! Jake!"

Sheriff Harris shook his head at Dunbar, as if to say, "What can I do?" He walked down the gazebo steps, just as Nina Wallace came up them and thrust her wand mike in front of Dunbar's face.

"Mayor Dunbar, why are you stopping this rally? Are you afraid of your opponent?"

Dunbar appeared speechless and choleric. I leaned into him.

"It's dog eat dog, Dunbar."

Dunbar looked out at the unfriendly crowd, then slunk down the gazebo steps.

Interlude

KTRS *Headline News* Report:
Dog Days in Erie, Colorado

Headline News anchorman Ed O'Brien twinkles for the camera. "A running dog is nothing new—unless he's running for office. That's exactly what one canine is doing in the town of Erie, Colorado—running for Mayor. Our Nina Wallace has the story."

Shot of Main Street: Jake, accompanied by Ken Miller, walks west on the north sidewalk, greeted by all passersby.

"This cute dog's name is Jake," Nina says off camera. "Just a week ago, he was basically homeless. That's when political advisor Ken Miller nearly ran him over outside of town. Ken saw something special in Jake. And today, the dog is a registered candidate for Erie mayor, and he's learned all the tricks of the campaign trail."

Natty hair stylist Bobby Davison stops and reaches over to pet Jake on the head. Jake instead offers Bobby his right paw. Bobby happily shakes the paw.

Jake and Miller approach a canopied baby stroller and proud young mother Helen McNee. Jake stands up on his hind legs, his front paws on the stroller. Helen lifts her baby boy from the carriage and shows him to Jake. Jake licks the baby's face, making him giggle.

Jake and Miller approach the Shaw Development Company office. Two posters in the window vie for attention. One is the El Dorado promo (*Where Treasures Meet Pleasures*), the other has a grinning Dunbar above the quote, *"The future of Erie looks bright as gold!"—Charles Dunbar, Erie Mayor.*

"Jake's platform is a simple one," says Nina's voice. "Stop a multimillion-dollar shopping mall/amusement park hybrid, which some Erie residents fear will end their small town tranquility. It's a project being pushed by incumbent mayor Charles Dunbar. And Jake has a clear message for him."

Jake pauses beside the window wall, right under the Dunbar poster. He raises his right hind leg and fires off a long stream. Miller looks suitably embarrassed, and hurries away with Jake.

Inside the Jake for Mayor Campaign Headquarters, Jake is seen sitting on a table top, studying a cardboard sheet held up by Miller. It shows a steeply rising graph line beneath the words, ERIE TAXES UNDER MAYOR DUNBAR. Jake snaps at the cardboard, pulling it down to the table, where he chews it to shreds.

Nina Wallace, resembling a fashion model for ski wear, stands outside Jake campaign headquarters, wand mike in hand. "But Jake's opponent also knows how to play to a camera. He's former TV star Charles Dunbar, better known as Big John Harrow from the nineties' hit show, *Empire*. Dunbar has been the mayor of Erie for eight years."

A smug Charles Dunbar speaks into Nina's wand mike. "It's just a silly protest vote against El Dorado, by the few people in town who prefer to live in the past century. Not the Twentieth Century—the Nineteenth."

Nina addresses the camera. "So while Jake is very much the under-dog, he has been winning some irresistible support."

An adorable little girl, 7, talks into Nina's mike. "I want mommy and daddy to vote for Jake 'cause he's cute and fluffy, just like my dog, Boomer."

Grumpy old man Fred Urich talks into Nina's mike. "I ain't cast a vote since Clinton said he didn't have sex with that woman. Least Jake's one politician who won't lie to us. He may not say much, but he won't lie. He's got my vote."

Cut back to Main Street, with Nina Wallace addressing the camera. "Those sentiments appear to be spreading. With one week to go in the race, more and more Erie residents say they're leaning toward Jake and against the incumbent. So if it's true that every dog has his day, Jake's just might be Election Day. This is Nina Wallace for *Headline News*."

Part II

DOGFIGHT

Chapter 17

I surveyed my kingdom in the wilderness with some guilt.

Our temporary campaign office was the permanent Erie Bingo Hall on Main Street, thanks to Jenny's soft-spoken yet formidable mother. Ruth Perkins had convinced her senior fast crowd that working phones for three weeks would be a fun change of pace from bridge. The rectangular room was furnished with two long wooden tables, each with eight green vinyl chairs on a single side, the aisle side clear. The aisle ran to the bingo caller's table, my desk for three more days. We'd bought eight landline phones and put one in front of every other chair, plus a laser printer by my desk. And we still had eight hundred dollars left in the coffer.

We all wore Jake for Mayor T-shirts and campaign buttons. Ruth and three of her girlfriends manned the left table (while two more sold T-shirts outside), my Jake Youth had the right table. Annie sat next to Alex, as usual, although separated by an empty chair (to reduce cross phone interference); she closer to my desk. Jake snored under the table at Alex's feet.

Jake for Mayor

My volunteer staff viewed our campaign as a moral crusade, and their dedication was paying off. *Fox and Friends* had cited the Jake story, and it was an internet viral hit, thankfully not yet as a joke. That would come on Election Day one week away. Jake would get a ridiculously high number of votes, way too few to beat Dunbar and stop El Dorado, yet more than enough to rescue my reputation at the expense of Erie's. Hence my guilt.

While awaiting an email from Greg Foster, I observed Alex and Annie on the phones.

"Fifty dollars, got it," said Alex. "Thanks a lot, Mrs. Hartley. I'll drop by around six to pick it up.... Mom's great. She'll see you in church Sunday." He hung up and wrote the name and figure on a sheet.

Annie was still on the phone, looking cutely skeptical. "How much?... One million, huh. How many zeroes in a million?... Well if you can't count to six, how'd you get to a million?... Nice try, Joey. Tell your dad to call in, okay?... Bye, Joey."

Annie hung up and turned to Alex. "Joey Henderson. He's got a crush on me."

"He's like eleven."

"He's very mature for his age."

"Yeah, I heard he's got his own paper route," Alex said with a smile.

"Well, some older boys wouldn't know a good thing if it bit 'em on the nose. The prize won't be around forever; I can tell you that right now."

Alex's smile vanished. "Where might it go?"

"Maybe St. Agnes High School in Denver."

Alex frowned. Annie's phone rang. She didn't answer it, just kept looking at Alex. *Say something, stupid,* I thought. The phone rang again. Neither Annie nor Alex budged, but Jake did under the table, awoken by the ceaseless ringing. He howled at the slack phone cable that ran under the tabletop. The phone rang a fifth time. That did it for Jake. He bit into the phone cord and pulled. The phone slid off the table and onto the vacant chair between the two kids. The receiver fell under the table, almost to the aisle.

Annie and Alex simultaneously ducked under the table to retrieve the receiver. With their faces close to one another's, Alex seemed to steel himself. *Do it,* I thought, *now or never.* Alex moved his mouth toward Annie's. She closed her eyes. Their lips pressed gently together and held there. Jake curiously observed the boy and girl kissing.

A faint female voice came through the receiver. "Hello? Hello? Someone there? Am I on hold? Where does Jake stand on women's rights? Hello?"

Annie opened her eyes, her cheeks slightly redder.

"Was that a good thing?" asked Alex.

Annie smiled, took the receiver and withdrew to her seat.

"Jake for Mayor," she said into the phone.

Alex remained under the table, now making eye contact with Jake. "What do you think?"

Jake moved out from the table to my desk and lay down at the foot of it. The email inbox dinged on my computer. It was a message from Greg Foster at US Senator Walter Atwood's website. I read some of it.

Jake for Mayor

Ken, baby, been following your news. Jesus, you're really doing it. A dog for Mayor! Way to put one over on them hillbillies. Hee haw. The Senator's really impressed. Naturally, the better your candidate does on E-Day, the better you'll look to him.

BTW, seeing as you're so chummy with the yokels, maybe you can earn some brownie points with my boss. We can't seem to raise his approval among the guns and Bible crowd. Could you add a few helpful lines to the following speech? Consider it an entrance exam. Hee haw, and chat soon.

The rest of the email body was a proposed speech by Senator Atwood. I preferred to read a hard copy of it. I pressed "print" and instantly cursed my stupidity, even before I saw Jenny walking up the aisle toward me and the printer. If she read just one of Greg's jabs at her people, so freely shared with me, I'd be finished, along with my comeback. And the document was halfway out the printer gate.

Like every weeknight at this time, Jenny wore her waitress uniform and bore a cardboard tray full of Miner's Diner's sandwiches for our campaign team. She placed the penultimate sandwich before Annie then approached me with mine, just as the paper shot out from the printer and floated down toward Jake's head. Jenny paused to watch the falling sheet. I rushed out from behind my table and got in front of her.

"Here let me help you with that," I said, pulling on Jenny's tray and leading her to my table.

"It's not heavy, Ken." She nodded at the paper on the floor. "Aren't you going to get that?"

"In a minute. I'm so hungry I could eat a horse."

"You're in luck. That's today's special."

I put the tray on the table and indicated a spot for Jenny. She jumped lithely backward onto the tabletop. I did the same on her left, our legs touching. Out of my left eye I saw Jake sniffing at the printout sheet. Let it go, I thought.

"You alright?" Jenny asked. "You seem nervous."

"Just excited. Your lovely self?"

"To be perfectly honest, Ken, I feel great. Better than I have in a long time. And I owe it all to you."

"Oh come on," I said, eying Jake.

Jake bit on the printout and brought it to me in his teeth.

"I mean it," Jenny said. "You kinda changed my life. And Alex's. In fact, this whole town's."

"It's all Jake, really."

I brought my left hand down to knee level, and surreptitiously waved Jake away.

"Jake's just a dog. You made him special. A symbol of something I thought we'd lost: town pride."

Jake looked up at me with the printout in his teeth. I made a grab for it, and Jake stepped back playfully. I turned to Jenny, as if in rapt attention, hoping she'd ignore Jake's catch.

"I got a confession to make," said Jenny.

"You might want Reverend Sloane."

To my horror, Jake got between Jenny's ankles, proffering her the printout sheet. She was too focused on me to notice. I could feel sweat on my forehead.

"Till last week, I took you for a no-good con man."

"That stings—I mean hurts."

"At first I thought—don't laugh—that it was my bod you were after."

"Don't discount that one so fast."

Jake, fed up with being ignored, dropped the paper at Jenny's feet, print side up, and went back to the volunteers' table.

"But you've been the perfect knight," said Jenny.

"I'm better in the morning."

I put my right shoe tip on the printout and slid it toward me, trying not to backslide off the table.

"Then I reckoned it was the donation money you were going for."

"Hey, eight hundred bucks is quite a haul."

I slid the printout closer with my shoe, but then lost it under Jenny's feet.

"But you put every last dime into the campaign. So I come to the conclusion that you, Ken Miller, are the real deal. Someone who cares about us folk. And I'm very glad you came along."

"Me too," I said without prevarication, surprising myself.

Jenny finally noticed the printout at her feet. She seemed about to pick it up. I put my left hand on her chin and turned her face toward mine. Seeing the invitation on it, I pressed my mouth against hers. Jenny returned the pressure. We kissed hard and well.

The room applauded. We broke off the kiss and waved to everybody.

"I better get back to work," Jenny said.

We stepped over the printout on the way to the door. We kissed again, more lightly this time. Jenny exited. I let out a long breath of relief. I scooped up the printout, tore it to shreds and threw them in the trash bin.

Chapter 18

Jenny and I walked hand in hand on the riverside path, occasionally behind Jake, who kept zipping after birds and squirrels. It was a cold grey Sunday morning, two days before Election Day. Sun rays broke through the cloud cover over the mountain range on our distant left. We were dressed for church.

Jenny had postponed consummating our romance until after the election, suspecting (rightly) that I'd be leaving Erie soon afterward. My argument that greater physical affection on her part could sway my decision fell on deaf ears, so handholding and kissing were as far as she went. Yet somehow she was still scoring points with me.

This day she brought up her late husband for the first time.

"Don's family owned our farm for near a hundred years. His dream was to leave it to Alex, and spend a chunk of his life working it with him. But when Nine-Eleven happened, Don took up his other family tradition. He joined the Marines. Alex wasn't even born then."

"But they got to see each other, right?"

"Sure. Three times in person, the rest on Skype, Don from Afghanistan or Iraq. Two weeks before his last tour ended, his hummer got blown up... along with my heart."

"I'm sorry," I said.

"We did good, considering. I married my childhood sweetheart. Alex had a hero dad."

"Those are some big shoes to fill," I said.

Jenny nodded.

"Mine are nine and a half."

Jenny smiled endearingly.

We reached the churchyard at first bell. It rang five more times while I leashed an uncooperative Jake to a steel bench leg, then thrice more as I walked into church with Jenny.

She left me in the foyer with a peck on the lips and climbed the stairs to the balcony. I continued up the aisle, past full pews of dark mahogany, and took a middle-right seat on the aisle. I looked back at the balcony, to see Jenny join the Donner brothers. Nick sat at the piano, John stood with his guitar. They began to play a dreamy tune that I almost recognized, then did when Jenny began to sing angelically. It was an old Cat Stevens song my mom loved. I never knew it had a religious angle.

> "Morning has broken, like the first morning,
> Blackbird has spoken, like the first bird.
> Praise for the singing,
> Praise for the morning,
> Praise for them springing, fresh from the world."

Jake for Mayor

This was the third church service in a row I'd attended, more to be seen than saved. Yet the homespun Reverend Sloane's smart, short sermons had rather grown on me. The full pews were absent Dunbar, a good thing too, since I'd been invited to speak from the pulpit, with one limitation. I addressed it early in my talk, using the country-speak I'd mastered during my three weeks in Erie.

"My new friends, in just two days you'll be casting a vote for Mayor, making a choice between not just two candidates, but two totally different roads for this town. Now, if I were to suggest which candidate God might prefer, some fancy judge in Denver would raise hel... ah, heck."

I saw smiles throughout the congregation.

"He'd cite some mysterious wall between Church and State that's nowhere to be found in the Constitution. So I'll just say this: one election result will make history. The other will end it, at least for Erie."

There were a few disturbed murmurs.

"Now some of you might think voting for a dog to be a bit silly. Reminds me of a parable, not in the Bible. A priest was standing in front of his church, when he saw a young man walking up the road to him. 'Excuse me, Father,' said the man. 'My dog just died, and I was hoping you could say a Mass for him.' The priest said, 'I'm sorry, my son, but dogs don't have a soul, so I'm afraid I can't help you.' 'I see,' said the man. 'Then could you recommend a church that might?' 'Well,' said the priest, 'There's a new church up the road. They may be more flexible.' 'Thank you, Father. I really loved that dog. Do you think a donation of ten-thousand dollars will be enough?' 'Just a minute,' said the priest. 'Was your dog Catholic? Why didn't you say so? Of course I'll say a Mass for him.'"

Raucous laughter answered me.

"Thank you all," I said. "Don't forget to vote on Tuesday."

After the service, I waited for Jenny by the stairway. People exited past me to her stirring rendition of "Lord of the Dance":

"I danced in the morning when the world was young,
I danced in the moon and the stars and the sun,
I came down from heaven and I danced on the earth,
At Bethlehem I had my birth."

Jenny came downstairs and took my hand. It felt more electric than some sexual contact I'd had with other women. We held hands all the way to the churchyard. Jake saw us and stood up, pulling on his leash. I began to untie him, then saw Rancher Sam strutting toward me like John Wayne on the way to a gunfight.

"Howdy, Sam," said Jenny, with a hint of concern on her face.

"Jenny," Sam said, glaring at me.

I slipped Jake's leash from the bench leg. "Something I can do for you, sir?"

"That dog of yours done enough already," Sam said.

Jenny looked distraught, as if she knew the cause of his belligerence.

"I'm sorry?"

"Your dog messed up my dog."

"Messed up? That fine collie of yours?"

"At that political rally three weeks back."

"Oh right," I said. "That little dog chase. Was Jake too rough with her? You'll have to excuse him, sir. Jake's quite the hound."

Jenny winced.

"Listen to me, boy. Tara's the best ranch hand I got. When I'm out on the range, she keeps the cattle in line and coyotes at bay."

"Really?" I said. "Never heard of a cow-dog before."

"You ain't catching my drift. Tara's no good to me in her condition."

Jenny cringed.

"I'll tell you what, sir," I said. "The campaign will pay for any special procedure by a vet."

"Ken," said Jenny, clearly worried.

I looked at her.

"When I caught up to Jake that day, he and Tara were... the opposite of fighting."

I finally got it. "Oh no. You mean to say she's...?"

"Yep," said Sam.

"I was afraid of that," said Jenny.

I looked accusingly at Jake. He cast down his eyes.

"That's all we needed—a sex scandal! How could you this to me?!" I turned to Sam. "I'm sorry about this, Sam."

"My friends call me Sam. You call me Mr. McKenna."

"Mr. McKenna, let's discuss this. I'm sure we can work something out. How much to keep this quiet?"

"I don't want money, boy. I was gonna fix that windmill today, while my son and Tara drove the herd up to

Centennial. Now I gotta do that. Which still leaves the windmill."

"I'll pay for a windmill repairman."

"T'ain't none around, 'specially on Sunday."

"Ken'll do it," said Jenny.

"Sure," I said. "How hard can it be to repair a... hey, wait a minute!"

Sam said, "Him? He's a tenderfoot. Look at his hands. He ain't never held a hammer in his life."

"He's right," I said.

"He's a good man, Sam, 'neath all the snake oil," said Jenny.

I stared at her.

"I'll take your word for it, Jenny," Sam said, looking askance at me. "Be at my ranch house in two hours. Don't be late, boy, or I'll come looking for you. And next time I won't be so friendly."

He strode away. I turned to Jenny.

"Thanks a lot."

"I'm thinking good, Ken. All the ranchers and farmers look up to Sam. You stay on his bad side, we're done for. 'Sides, it'll make a good—what you call it?" Jenny snapped an invisible camera. "Photo op. You and Jake working on a ranch."

"I've created a monster," I said.

Chapter 19

The McKenna windmill rose just under 30 feet above rich grassland a mile northwest of the ranch house. Timber posts leaned into each other to link at the top point, where spun a dozen aluminum blades. The posts were linked at three levels by wood crossbeams, twelve in all, the greater the height, the shorter the beams. All the beams had rotted, and they needed replacing by the last person imaginable, me.

I stood on a steel hook ladder with a crowbar in hand, prying loose the last of the four highest beams. Four yards behind me and about the same distance down was a hot tub fit for Paul Bunyan, actually the cistern that the windmill would fill with underground water. I had taken off my coat despite the grey day's chill, having never sweated so much outside of a workout, with or without Sharon.

On a small mount in the nearby grass, my digital camera sat peering up at me. It would snap a photo every ten minutes to record my carpentry progress and provide a nice picture for the *Erie Gazette* on Election Day morning. "Ken Miller, Jake for Mayor Campaign Manager, helps out a local rancher." Jake lay near the camera, chewing on his second raw T-bone of the day.

"Hey, Jake," I said, pulling hard on the crowbar against a resistant beam. "I hope you're not getting too tired munching on that bone."

I felt the beam start to loosen and yanked on the crowbar with full might. The board came out all at once, and sent me flying backward toward my doom. The camera clicked to record the precise moment of my death.

I fell into the cistern with a splash. My relief at being alive soon turned to fear of freezing in the icy water. I caught a handhold on the wall, then two more above it, and climbed to the cistern's top rim. Jake was barking at me, either in concern or mockery, his front paws on the cistern wall. I dangled from the rim and dropped to the grass, then sat with my back against the tank. Jake eagerly licked my face.

"Stop it, will you? I'm wet enough already," I said.

I looked at the stack of new crossbeams near the windmill base, then at the hammer and box of nails beside it, and finally up at the beamless structure.

"You know, Jake, taking down those old beams was the easy part. And that nearly killed me. So how am I expected to put up the new ones? Sam McKenna was right. I suck at real work. My only skill is persuading content people that they're discontent, and that contentment comes from something, or someone, beyond themselves. Hell of an epitaph, huh? Well, dog, I'm not dead yet. I can do one real job in my life, even if it's on a windmill in the middle of nowhere."

I stood up and approached the wood stack, then took up the hammer.

Two hours later, I nailed in the last crossbeam. My wet clothes had dried from the combination of physical exertion and sunlight. I came down the ladder, and Jake greeted me at the foot of it. I saw Sam McKenna riding toward me on his great white steed. He stopped the horse in front of us and unstrung a small burlap sack behind him. He lowered the clearly heavy weight with one hand then let it drop on the grass.

"Here's the cement."

"Cement, right," I said. "Uhm, what do I do with it?"

"Pour around them posts to shore up the base."

I glanced at the four slabs of cracked concrete around the windmill's grass-deep leg posts.

"Got it," I said.

McKenna turned his mount rightward and rode past my left. The horse trotted slowly around the windmill, pausing intermittently so that his rider could inspect my handiwork. I was sure he'd find it deficient, and I awaited his scorn.

"You done good," he said, circling back to me.

I felt like I'd won an Olympic Gold Medal.

"To tell you the truth, I didn't think you could do it."

"It was a safe bet," I said.

"All you got left is the foundation. Take your time there. Without a strong foundation, the Leaning Tower would'a been the Fallen Tower long ago."

I stared at McKenna in surprise.

"Don't look so amazed, son. I been abroad. Lot of us old hicks have. Saw the sights, though mostly jungle and guts."

"Vietnam," I said, recalling my Green Beret Uncle Matt's brutal tales of the war.

"Three round trips. Some I knew just went one way. Anyways, good job."

"Thanks, Mr. McKenna."

"Call me Sam."

I smiled. Sam turned his horse around, and rode off at a gallop.

"Yee ha," I said with a grin, and picked up the sack of cement powder.

Chapter 20

I sat on two dead planks chugging a bottled water while waiting for Jenny to pick up Jake and me. My arms felt like I'd driven in a chariot race against Ben Hur. Jake lay sprawled near me as if he'd done the windmill repair work. I was glad to see the old white pickup truck speeding toward us, until I remembered Jenny's truck was green.

Four burly men stood in the truck bed, three wearing flannel shirts, one an orange cap. I recognized Orange Cap as Hank, the surveyor Jenny almost ran over on her farm. These had to be El Dorado workmen, I deduced.

I rose to my feet. Jake snarled as the truck came to a stop in front of us. The workmen jumped down to the grass, two on each side of the truck. All four wore construction boots and jeans. They didn't advance, just glared at me. In politics, when your opponent tries to intimidate you, you need to deflate him fast. A little false bravado was in order.

"What's this—a Chippendales act? Please leave the pants on."

The truck's driver's door opened. Ry Coogan got out and approached me with a smirk. I stood my ground. Jake growled, bearing his teeth.

"Remember me, boy?"

"Like my last toothache," I said.

"You and that dog have caused me a lotta grief."

"By promising a new literacy law?"

"Use to be just Jenny. Now more townsfolk wanna end our job."

I shook my head. "Just Mayor Dunbar's."

"His money men are gettin' cold feet."

"They'll be frozen stiff by Tuesday," I said.

"No they won't, 'cause Dunbar's gonna win the election. Know why? I remembered that mutt was mine after all."

"Bull! You were going to shoot him down like a—you're lying!"

"So me and my men are takin' 'im back."

Ry whistled through his teeth. The workmen moved toward us. Jake by my side barked menacingly at them. One fuzzy-faced man bent down to snatch him. I shoved his chest, knocking him on his butt. Two other men grabbed my arms. The fourth, Hank, punched me in the stomach, knocking the wind out of me and replacing it with pain. Hank pulled his fist back to slug my jaw but shrieked when Jake bit his left ankle. Hank tried to hit him, but Jake ran away.

Ry yelled, "Get the dog!"

"Run, Jake!" I said, short of breath and struggling against my holders.

Jake ran twenty feet and spun around to bark at the workmen. Hank started toward him then groaned, favoring his left ankle.

"Go ahead," I said. "Jake always chews up both chicken legs."

Hank turned back to me, but Ry stopped him.

"Forget him! Get the mutt!"

Hank resumed the chase for Jake. My two restrainers unhanded me to join the hunt. I fell to my knees, holding my stomach, and watched their maneuvers.

The workmen tried to dragnet Jake, but he kept darting between and around them, wrecking their formation. Fuzzy dove at him and fell on his face when Jake dashed away. Jake went a safe distance and continued his barking. Ry drew a beef jerky out of his jeans' back pocket and held it out to Jake.

"Here ya go, pooch. Nice fresh meat. You know you love it."

Jake quit barking and stared at Ry. Ry stood in place, proffering the stick of beef, but gave his workmen a subtle nod. They spread out in opposite directions to sweep the dog.

"Don't fall for it, Jake," I said, barely audibly, still having difficulty breathing.

Jake moved two steps closer to Ry. The workmen closed in behind him from both sides. Jake seemed oblivious to them, intent on the jerky stick in Ry's hand. I could hardly bear to watch as Jake chomped on the jerky and began wolfing it down. Fuzzy ran in on Jake's right and grabbed him by the neck. Jake bucked and growled, to no avail.

"Someone's comin', boss!" Hank called.

"Let's git!" said Ry.

Fuzzy carried Jake to the truck. The other three workmen followed. Ry approached me, the smirk back on his face.

"Got a message for ya from the Mayor," Ry said.

He punched me in the jaw, knocking me on my left side. I saw him run to his truck. Jake's head hung over the rear hatch, staring sadly at me. The truck sped away and shrank into the distance. I shut my eyes.

I heard a second vehicle motor approach, then two doors open and shut. A pair of shapely legs under a denim skirt knelt down in front of me.

"Ken, are you all right?!" Jenny asked anxiously.

"They took Jake," I said. "Coogan and his men."

"Bastards!" said Alex, appearing behind Jenny.

"Help me get 'im up," Jenny told her son.

Alex grabbed me by the armpits, Jenny by the wrists. They pulled me to my feet with a slight assist from me.

"I can stand," I said.

The Garrets released me.

"Let's get you to Doc Pritchard," said Jenny.

"No. I got to save my candidate."

"I'll call Sheriff Toby."

"Do it while you drop me off."

"Where?"

"El Dorado, and fast, Jenny."

"It's Sunday. There's no construction going on there."

"Just *destruction*—of Jake."

I hurried to the truck, flanked by the Garrets. Jenny jumped into the driver's seat. I got in on the passenger side, then Alex on my right. Jenny drove off in the same direction as Ry's truck, toward El Dorado. Alex reached behind the seat and pulled out his backpack. Jenny eyed him with concern.

"Whatcha gonna do with that?"

"We practice hockey at that site on weekends. It's got smooth floors like ice."

"That's trespassing," said Jenny. "How do you get in?"

"The side fence ends at the river," Alex said, more to me than Jenny. "We can go around it. I'll show you."

"No, Alex, it's too dangerous," Jenny said.

"Your mom's right," I said, rubbing my jaw. "Those guys play rough."

"Am I still Jake's Secret Service?"

"Sure."

"Then it's my job."

I looked at Jenny. On her face, pride fought with worry, and won. She nodded.

"Let's go get Jake," I said.

Chapter 21

Jenny pulled off the road near the northwest corner of a tall wire fence, barbed on top. The main fence continued alongside the road for about a half mile farther, the side fence a quarter mile rightward to the river, bordered by thick woods. A patchy grass field within the fence was dominated in back by the long steel and concrete exoskeleton of El Dorado. Parked near the far midsection was a cement truck, and beside it, the white pickup.

"They're here," I said.

"Ken, please wait for Toby," said Jenny. "He'll be getting back to us any minute."

"Any minute could be Jake's last," I said. "You come with the cavalry."

Alex got out of the truck and slipped into his backpack. Jenny and I remained in the cab, her green eyes boring into me.

"You'll look after my boy?"

"I will. And myself."

Jenny moved her lovely mouth to mine and gave me a delectable kiss.

"Wow," I said. "Any more where that came from?"

"It's a promise."

I got out of the truck. The sun had sunk below the treetops, leaving less than an hour of daylight. Alex led me along the tree-lined fence toward the river. The closer we got the louder it churned. The fence ended at a rock cliff overlooking the river, but stuck out a foot past the cliff edge. Alex grabbed the end fencepost with both hands then straddled it, his back overhanging the river twenty feet below.

"If you die, I'll die," I said.

"You'll miss me that much?"

"No, your mom'll kill me."

Using the fence links as handholds, Alex pulled himself to safety on the opposite side, then waved at me to join him. I took a deep breath and tried to duplicate his maneuver. It was like crossing the Berlin Wall—only into East Berlin. I managed the acrobatic feat.

Fully exposed inside enemy territory, we ran along the riverside toward the El Dorado structure. A concrete boardwalk protruded from the second story level for a quarter of its length, the outer edge above the river. This was to be El Dorado's outdoor restaurant row, the scenic river view a draw. We reached the west back corner of the building and took cover under the boardwalk, next to a temporary wooden staircase.

Alex said, "We know they're in there."

"And up to no good."

Alex took off his backpack and laid it on the ground. He kicked off his sneakers and withdrew his rollerblades from the knapsack.

"What are you doing?"

"I'll distract 'em while you grab Jake," Alex said.

"They'll grab *you*."

"After a little runaround."

He stuck his right leg into the rollerblade boot.

"Forget it, dude."

"Ken, say they do catch me. I'm just a rollerblading kid—Jenny's brat. The worst they'll do to me is kick me out. You they might shoot."

I tried to counter his Vulcan logic but failed. "Alright, we'll play it your way."

Alex clamped down his rollerblades. We ascended the lumber staircase, Alex rather awkwardly, given his slippery footwear and the gap under each step, to emerge on the concrete boardwalk. It was about forty yards long, with a single wooden handrail to keep careless workmen from a long drop into the river on the right. The boardwalk ended at a left-bound corridor. I looked down at the river, now reflecting the last rays of sunshine.

"Got any idea where Jake might be?" I asked.

Alex pointed to the left-bound corridor at boardwalk's end. "There's a construction office down that way."

"Okay," I said, then another word popped out of my head. "Corral."

We traveled down the boardwalk, Alex circling me on his rollerblades. He was quite expert, even rolling backwards.

118

We reached the end of the boardwalk and made a left onto the corridor, into the bowels of El Dorado.

We were in a roofless walkway, half a football field long, between two rows of plywood walls demarking future shops. This was one of four corridors intersecting the main one, visible ahead at midpoint. Our walkway doubled as a storage area for construction equipment. We passed two adjacent aluminum drainage pipes, maybe fifty feet long by three feet in circumference, and several power cables. Further on by the right wall stood a yellow forklift, beyond it a chest-high stack of plywood.

Alex pointed at the right corner of the walkway and main corridor. Just past the plywood stack was a lumber wall with a door in it. We approached the corner, Alex gliding ahead of me. We were halfway to the door when it swung open. Alex zipped behind the stack of plywood as I ducked behind the forklift. Hank and Fuzzy Face came out of the doorway, leaving the wooden door inwardly ajar. They turned left and walked directly toward our hiding spots, Fuzzy Face studying a smartphone in his hand.

"Ten zip Broncos. Think we'll get to see the second half?"

"Hope so," said Hank. "How long's it take to smoke a frickin' dog?"

"That ain't our job."

"Why, we're workin' overtime today."

They approached the far side of the plywood stack. Alex crouched behind the near end, his back to me, about to be spotted by the workmen. Just as they reached the far end of the stack, Alex, still in his crouch, rolled silently to the plywood wall then squeezed himself between it and the boards. The men walked obliviously by the stack, but now

119

straight toward my forklift. I held my breath as they passed me en route to the boardwalk, their voices fading.

"What if Sheriff Harris shows up? You heard Ry. That city boy we stomped must a gone crying to him by now."

"Dunbar'll take care of Harris. We just gotta give 'im a heads up."

I watched them reach the boardwalk and exit right, then joined Alex beside the plywood stack.

"Did you hear that?" Alex whispered.

"Yeah," I whispered back. "Dunbar's behind this. And Jake's on borrowed time."

"We gotta save 'im, Ken."

"We will. Wait here 'til I tell you."

We left our plywood hideout and skulked toward Ry's office, my cowardice only superseded by fear for Jake. A few feet from the doorway, I heard a familiar snarling sound. I crossed to the other side of the ajar door, ready for a quick dart around the corner. Ry's voice came through loud and clear.

"Why don't I just snap his neck and save a bullet?"

I peered through the door crack. On the dusty floor, near a rickety wooden table, a despondent Jake lay between two pairs of sitting pant legs, Coogan's jeans and Dunbar's khakis, a black choke collar around his neck.

"That would make it worse," said Dunbar.

Jake growled, but at a lower ebb than normal. I shuddered to think what they'd done to him.

"The mutt's a local media darling, and my celebrity opponent. People see a broken neck on 'im, you can forget about my election, start worrying about my execution."

Jake growled weakly.

"So what do we do with 'im?"

"I'll ask Max Shaw. He'll be calling me back shortly, before some big video conference."

Jake growled.

"Shaw working this late on a Sunday?"

"It's Monday morning in Australia."

Another weak growl escaped Jake.

"I'm going to the john," said Dunbar. "If that dog moves a muscle, kick 'im."

Jake growled again. Dunbar's chair creaked as he stood up. I ran back to the plywood stack and hid beside Alex. The makeshift door opened wider as Dunbar left the office. He turned right toward the main corridor, then right again, out of sight.

"Now or never," said Alex.

"Right."

We left our plywood hideout and approached the door. I didn't relish the prospect of fighting Ry but saw no other option. We were almost to the door when a cellphone rang in the office. I paused, as did Alex next to me. If I rushed in now, the person on the other end might hear and call for reinforcements. On the other hand, Dunbar would be back any moment. It was a lose-lose dilemma. Alex resolved it. He dashed past the door to the other side. From his position he could check the main corridor for Dunbar's return.

"Mayor Dunbar's phone," said an unfamiliar gruff voice.

I gulped. There was another man in the room. And I'd been about to charge in there like Batman. I'd done a boxing workout in college, but hitting a heavy bag at the

Northwestern gym was not fighting two construction workers. The phone rang again.

"Crap," Ry said. "Put it on speaker. Hello?"

"Dunbah?" a deep, commanding voice boomed through the cellphone speaker, his Australian accent evident in the dropped "r". "Max Shaw here."

Jake let out a faint growl. Alex and I exchanged looks.

"Mr. Shaw," said Ry. "It's a great honor."

"Stuff it, mate. Where's Dunbar? This call's costing me a merger."

"He'll be back in a minute, sir."

"I don't have a minute. Dunbah said you're having dog trouble. And that this dog is—did I hear him right—*running for Mayor?*"

"That's right, sir. Dog's been turnin' all the townsfolk against us."

"Crikey. No wonder your country's going down the tubes. Where's the dingo now?"

Another weak growl from Jake.

"Right here, sir. But killin' 'im 'll raise a ruckus. The dog's gotten kinda famous."

"We can make that work for us. There are fish in that river of yours, right?"

"Yes, sir, real big ones."

"All right. Here's what you do. Drown the dingo in the river. Everyone'll think he fell in and became fish food."

Jake growled.

"Dunbah will announce a fishing contest in his memory. Your locals will appreciate the gesture, and vote for him on Tuesday. Got the idea, mate?"

Jake growled again.

"I sure do, Mr. Shaw. And let me say, your plan is pure genius—"

"Stuff it."

"He hung up," Ry said. "No wonder I ain't been promoted. I been too nice a guy. Grab our fish bait, Carl. I'll tell Dunbar the plan."

Alex peered into the main corridor. He turned to me and nodded. Dunbar was returning. We ran back to our plywood hideout and ducked behind it. Dunbar came around the corner and reentered the office.

"When they come out, I'll jump 'em," I said.

"Me too," said Alex.

"No. You've got to get Jake out of here, no matter what happens to me. Is that clear?"

"Yeah."

We waited nervously. The office door slid open. Dunbar and Ry came out, followed by Carl, one of the two workmen who'd held my arms while Hank punched me in the gut. Carl dragged Jake out through the doorway by a leash. Jake tried to resist, but the choke collar did its dirty work. Near me, Alex shook with rage and seemed about to expose himself. I gripped his arm, a bit too tightly. I was angry too.

Ry closed the door behind Jake. The men would either head our way or toward the main corridor, which would foil my surprise attack. Jake sensed something, and turned in my direction. When Carl pulled his leash again, he offered no resistance.

Alex and I ducked lower, me ready to strike. Then Jake gave me away. He barked weakly yet happily, and soon his beagle face appeared beside me. He barked again, yanking on his leash to reach me.

Carl came up behind Jake, a curious look on his pockmarked face. I tackled him. He fell on his back, with me on top of him, and let go of the dog leash. Dunbar and Ry appeared frozen in shock.

"Go, Alex!"

Alex emerged and snatched Jake's leash.

"Come on, Jake!"

He sped off on his rollerblades, pulling Jake toward the main corridor. They rounded the right corner and vanished from my view. Dunbar and Ry unfroze.

"Damn dog's getting away!"Dunbar yelled.

Ry almost ate his cellphone. "They're on the main walkway! Seal all exits!"

Beneath me, Carl struggled to get free. I kept his arms pinned, until a kick to my right side blasted me off him and into the plywood stack. Pain shot through my ribs. Ry stood over me with a furious expression. Carl stomped toward me, about to do me more damage.

"Git after the dog!" Ry said.

Carl turned and ran toward the main corridor. Dunbar appeared beside Ry. Both men stared daggers at me for a moment, then took off behind Carl.

I sat up against the plywood stack, pressing my hurt rib. I couldn't help Alex or Jake, only hope that they'd gotten out. To my left, I saw Hank, Fuzzy, and two more workmen approaching from the boardwalk end of the crosswalk. Then I heard something worse on my right, the whooshing of Alex's rollerblades getting louder and closer. He was still in the main corridor and coming back this way. They must have blocked his exits.

Jake rounded the near left corner into view, pulling Alex on his rollerblades like a water skier. They turned right into the crosswalk and came toward me. Alex nodded to me as they sped past, heading toward the boardwalk—and the closing four-man trap.

The nearest workman, Fuzzy, planted himself like a Sumo wrestler in the fleers' path, ready to jump either way to grab Jake. Dog and boy rushed right at him, seemingly easy prey. A few feet short of Fuzzy, Jake split left and Alex right, lowering the taut dog leash between them to almost floor level. The leash cut down Fuzzy at the ankles, knocking him flat on his face. Jake and Alex continued their flight, still blocked by the two workmen and, further back, Hank.

The twin broad drainage pipes beside the left wall narrowed the escape route even more. The two workmen took advantage of this and lined up with the center of the pipes, leaving little room for the escapees to get past them. Jake and Alex closed to twenty-five yards of the men, then cut left toward the drainage pipe blockade. Alex let go of the leash and leapt onto the pipe tops as Jake ran into the left pipe and vanished from sight.

Alex glided over the double pipes, past the two gaping workmen. Only Hank now stood in his path at the far end of the drainage pipes. Alex flew off the pipe tops and kicked out with his right leg. A rollerblade boot caught Hank in the chest, knocking him on his back. Alex landed on the floor without stopping, just as Jake emerged from the drainage pipe. They headed for daylight, dim now beyond the crosswalk.

I heard fast-moving footsteps on my right. Ry and Carl ran past me on the way to the boardwalk, followed by a huffing, power-walking Dunbar.

I had to do something to help my companions. Using the plywood behind me for support, I managed to stand up. I pressed my aching side and began jogging toward the boardwalk. I passed Hank, rising unsteadily to his feet. I stopped, returned to Hank, and threw a punch at his jaw. Hank went down. I resumed my painful jog toward the boardwalk.

I turned right on the boardwalk and gulped. Alex stood at mid-point, with Jake in his arms, barking at both sides of the boardwalk. On my side, Dunbar, Ry, Carl and the two workmen were closing in on Alex, while two more workmen approached from the opposite side.

"Don't move, son!" Dunbar said. "All we want is that dog!"

"Oh yeah?!" said Alex. "Well come and get 'im!"

He tucked Jake under one arm like a football and rollerbladed straight for the handrail. He ducked under the rail and flew a good way farther before plunging twenty feet to the river.

"No!" I cried.

I ran forward, plowing through Ry and Carl. I went under the handrail and dove into the dark river below. After what seemed like a minute, I hit water and sank. The bad news was the icy water. The good news was I forgot about my rib pain while I powered up to the surface. In the dim sunlight, I saw Jake some thirty feet away, frantically dog paddling. Alex was nowhere in sight. I swam hard and fast toward Jake, searching all around me for Alex.

I reached the fast paddling Jake and tapped his head. Jake ignored me for the first time ever. He swam away from me, circled back, and went past me again, still in a circle, and circled back. I soon realized what he was doing. I swam inside Jake's circle and dove straight down. I descended and into darker water, past the point of cold and fear, until I saw Alex.

He stood near the river bottom, his right foot on a branchy log, trying to propel himself up with desperate yet ineffective arm sweeps. I saw why they had no effect when I got close to him. His left rollerblade boot was caught between two thick branches so that he couldn't reach it. He was trying to thrust his way free, failing, and fading. He looked at me with terror.

I dove beneath the entrapping branches, took hold of his boot, and unsnapped all three clasps. Alex shot up to the surface like a Polaris missile. I ascended after him, and only a bit slower.

It was nearly dark. Alex had a hold of Jake in one arm, and was swimming toward shore with the other. I followed them in. A flashlight beam from the El Dorado side illuminated us. I almost wept. We hadn't drowned, but we were sunk.

"Alex?!" came a woman's voice.

"Mom!"

We swam toward Jenny's voice, Alex still lifeguarding Jake. The flashlight beam shut off, revealing two shadowy figures on the shore. I made out Jenny's curvaceous form and that of Sheriff Toby Harris. It was the only time he ever looked better to me than she did.

Chapter 22

I sat in Sheriff Harris' compact office with Alex, Jenny, and Deputy Gordon Smith, drinking creamy coffee in Styrofoam cups while describing the dognapping of Jake. The dog lay on the floor between two vinyl armchairs, bored by my account of his (this time) genuine heroics in the river. Jenny occupied another chair, her son its right armrest. Alex and I were dry, clean and warm after a pit stop at our places. I'd put on jeans, a green flannel shirt, and black running shoes.

Deputy Smith manned the Sheriff's desk, typing my report into a sleek desktop computer. He was a twenty-something ex-linebacker with short brown hair. Harris was still at El Dorado, interrogating the villains of my tale, Dunbar and Ry Coogan. I hoped they would continue their partnership in jail. Smith had just pressed "Print" on the report when a dour Sheriff Harris walked in alone. His deputy vacated the desk chair. Harris took the seat and blew air out through closed lips.

"What, no prisoners?" I said.

"Nope. Not gonna be, neither."

"How come, Toby?" asked Jenny.

"I got good news and bad news. Which do you wanna hear first?"

"The bad news," said Alex.

"Eight El Dorado workers said they didn't leave the site all day. And they'll swear to that in court."

"Of course," I said.

"You add Coogan and Dunbar to that list, it's ten against one."

"Me."

"Then how come they had Jake?" said Alex. "We heard 'em threatening to kill 'im."

"According to them, you and Miller brought the dog with you."

"Ten against two," I said.

"That's a lie," Jenny said. "I took 'em there to get Jake."

"All right, ten against three," said Sheriff Harris. "You got any more witnesses?"

I pointed to Jake.

"Sorry, Miller."

"What's the good news?" I asked.

"Dunbar ordered me to arrest you for trespassing."

"How is that good?"

"I said no. So come Tuesday, this town's either gonna have a new mayor, or a new Sheriff."

"I guess Jake's got your vote," I said.

It was nearly ten that PM when Jake and I got back to the hotel. I walked into what I thought was the wrong room. A compact blue suitcase lay open on the bed. The bathroom light was on, and the shower running. I left the room door half open for a rapid exit. Then I recognized the suitcase as the one Sharon had held when she walked out on me in Phoenix. While I pondered this, Sharon came out of the bathroom, almost busting out of a short pink cotton spa robe, with a seductive smile.

"Hello, sweetheart," Sharon said.

She embraced me and gave me a deep, wet kiss. Her moist hair smelled like fresh strawberries. Jake jumped on the bed and began sniffing the suitcase contents.

"I missed this," Sharon said, squeezing me.

"You're the one who discontinued it."

"I know, babe. How silly of me."

I backed up and sat down on the bedside. "What are you doing here, Shar?"

"Is that anyway to greet your fiancée?"

She sat down next to me, her firm, bare leg over my jeaned one.

"I've come to support you in your trial tomorrow, and the election the day after."

"You hung up on me the last time we talked. When I said I was running a dog for Mayor."

"I was angry, honey. I wanted you with me."

"In hell? That's where you told me to go."

"But not to stay," said Sharon, gesturing at the window and, I supposed, right outside it.

"Erie's alright. It's full of nice people."

"Most of them in *Duck Dynasty*. But I have to admit, Ken, you've made it work for you—and in politics, at that. I should never have doubted you."

Sharon's bra appeared between us, the deep right cup stuck in Jake's snout. I pulled it off, then put Jake on the floor.

"So this is Jake," said Sharon, stroking the pliant dog's head.

"For Mayor. How'd you know his name?"

"He made the Chicago news, too."

"Ah."

"Jake for Mayor," said Sharon. "It's brilliant. I'm proud of you, babe."

"I'm the comeback kid."

"That makes two of us."

Sharon pressed her lips to mine. I kissed back, my body working faster than my brain. So was my mouth, or I'd have kept it shut.

"Once Jake loses Tuesday, things'll move fast. He'll get plenty of votes, and I'll get the credit. Next stop, Washington DC. No more putting on the hicks for me. I'll be managing a real candidate instead of a stupid dog."

I felt a sudden chill at my spine. I knew the cause of it without turning around, but did anyway.

"Jenny."

She stood in the open doorway, her fierce green eyes darting from me to Sharon then back to me.

"Tell me you didn't just say that, Ken. I'll believe you. You proved you can sell this hick anything."

"I didn't mean you, Jenny."

"Part of me always knew you weren't for real. I kept wishing it down. But you're even worse than I thought. This whole time, you were using me, and my son, and my town. For what? A job?! You lying no good bastard!"

I bristled. "Listen, Jenny, who cares why I did it? Jake scores big tomorrow, El Dorado's dead. That is what you want, isn't it?"

"*I* care!" Jenny said. "I believed in you!"

"That was your problem," I said.

Jenny's eyes moistened. "I hope you can live with yourself —and your rich little tramp!"

She spun and left.

"How'd she know I'm rich?" said Sharon. "Ken. Were you cheating on me with Shania Twain?"

"No," I said, then felt a pang of regret. "No."

Jake looked at me, I could have sworn in accusation. It set me off. My blood was up after Jenny's moral reprimand.

"What are you looking at, mutt?! Who are you to judge me?! I made you! And if you don't like it, you can get out too!"

Jake surprised me once again. He turned around and walked out the door.

Chapter 23

I awoke with the first rays of sunlight, ready to walk Jake as usual. I reached for him on the bed beside me and felt Sharon's arm instead. She slept spooning me under the covers. The irony struck me. All the times I'd hoped it could be Sharon in my bed instead of Jake, and now I missed the latter. Sharon opened her bedroom eyes, smiled and stroked my chest.

"Good morning, sweetheart," she said. "Which one are you thinking about? Your trial today or the election tomorrow?"

"Mostly about Jake."

"Mmm, me too. Like you said, if that silly dog does well tomorrow, we'll be the next Washington power couple. I'll look great on your arm."

"What about my candidates?" I asked. "Will you care where they stand on the issues?"

"No more than you, babe. You'll tell them what to say."

"Whatever it takes to win," I said. "My credo for as long as I can remember. And what has it gotten me? Nothing I really care about. Till I came here, to Erie, Colorado, this tiny backwater community. You know, I never understood that word before: 'community'. But for a little while, I was part of one."

"You sure took advantage of it."

"Yeah," I said. "I sure did."

I rolled out of bed and approached the dresser. My wardrobe from last night lay on top of it, next to Sharon's suitcase. I started to get into my jeans.

"Where you going?"

"Just out for a walk."

"Bring me back a Frappuccino."

"There's no Starbucks in Erie, Shar. At least not yet. I'll bring you a normal cup of coffee."

I walked down Main Street in the frosty wind, looking around for Jake. I was anxious to see his canine face again, and not just because tomorrow was Election Day. Soon I saw it, but only on a Jake for Mayor flyer fluttering on a lamp post.

My search brought me to Jake Campaign headquarters. The bingo hall looked desolate, since our electioneering had concluded two days prior. As I neared the door, it swung open. Tommy and Pedro came out carrying cardboard boxes full of office equipment and apparel, followed by Alex and Annie, also bearing boxes. All four Jake Campaign Youth walked by me as in a funeral procession, without once glancing at the corpse—me.

Moving away, Alex stopped then turned to me. Annie duly did the same, supporting her boyfriend.

"He's at our farm," Alex said. "Case you're interested."

134

"Jake?"

"Mom brought 'im home last night."

"I'm glad."

"Sheriff Peters said for me to bring 'im to your trial today."

"Why?"

"He said Jake's part of it."

"My *trial*," I said. "Yeah, I guess he is."

"Will you tell me something?"

"Sure."

Alex nodded at the campaign office. "Was all this some kind of joke to you?"

"At first," I said. "Though not for some time. You kids made the difference. So did your mom. And Jake... Jake... well.... Take good care of 'im, Alex."

Alex turned away. He and Annie walked after their friends. I rubbed my eyes. The wind must have been wetter than I thought.

I resumed my odyssey, now toward Sam McKenna's ranch. Why there I didn't know. A half hour later, I looked up at the windmill I'd restored with my bare hands. It stood tall against the grey sky, blades spinning smoothly in the strong breeze. I didn't hear Sam McKenna or his collie come up behind me.

"The beams are crooked and the nails too far apart," said McKenna, appearing on my left with a steaming mug of coffee in his hand. "But I bet she's just about the handsomest thing you ever saw."

Tara lay down on the grass, clearly not at her best.

"Yeah," I said. "That it is."

Lou Aguilar

"It's hard work to build something up. Whole lot easier to tear it down. Me, I'll take hammer over sledgehammer any day. See ya around, boy."

I nodded. "Sam."

McKenna headed toward his ranch house. I started back to town.

I entered my hotel room to see Sharon standing before the bathroom door mirror, checking her array of brown stockings, short grey skirt and purple short-sleeve silk blouse. She turned to me and undulated sexily.

"How's this for the 'Concerned Fiancée' look? They won't dare convict you now. Keeping you away from *this* for any length of time would be cruel and unusual punish—"

"Shut up, Sharon."

Her luscious mouth fell open. "What did you say to me?"

"Better yet, go home. This town ain't big enough for the two of us."

"Oh, I get it," said Sharon. "You're planning to move to DC without me. Now that you're hot stuff."

"I'm not going to Washington. I'm staying right here, among real people. No matter what happens tomorrow."

"Come on, Ken! Three weeks in nowhere-ville and you've grown a conscience? It's that country wench you want. How long could you stand it here, even with her in your bed?"

"Denver's half an hour away. It has advertising firms too. I'll commute."

"You'll go mad. You forget, I know you, Mr. Smith Goes to Washington!"

"Not no more," I said.

"Fine. Stay here with your hillbilly friends. And your little dog too!"

I left the hotel room so that Sharon could pack. I hoped she would be fast. My trial was in less than an hour.

Chapter 24

The Erie Courtroom filled up fast. It was much broader than long, with six wooden bench rows on each side of the aisle, the prosecutor's table on the left row, defender's on the right. Behind an oak railing stood the vacant judge's bench, flanked by a sitting court reporter, a young American Indian woman, typing on her laptop, and the rigidly standing Deputy Smith.

I sat alone at the defender's table, casting furtive glances to my left. The prosecutor appeared outright vulturic—a lean, balding, middle-aged man wearing a grey suit, gold wire glasses and, naturally, a red bow tie. He was perusing a document on the table.

I wore my light blue Armani power suit with striped red tie. One should dress well for the gallows. I kept looking back at the spectator rows, hoping and yet dreading to see Jenny. I saw almost everyone I knew in town except for her, Alex and Jake. Sam McKenna was there, plus the two El Dorado investors: hotelier Noah Richards and banker Warren Boyle.

Directly behind the prosecutor, Mayor Dunbar caught my eye and smiled as if anticipating a death sentence. On his right, Ry Coogan directed a throat-cutting gesture at me. Those two were a regular Abbot and Costello.

Nina Wallace sat in the last right row by the aisle. She gave me a hypocritical thumb-up. We both knew a guilty verdict would make bigger news. Camera man Bill stood beside Nina and behind a tripod-mounted camcorder. Sheriff Harris sat at my back, three spaces in from the aisle. He appeared to be saving the other seats. I soon saw for whom.

Jenny entered the courtroom with Jake on his leash. Alex and Annie followed close behind, Alex holding what looked like a DVD case. The Garrets and Annie took the seats behind me. Jake sat on Jenny's lap. Neither of them looked at me.

"All rise," Deputy Smith said. "Court is now in session, the honorable Judge Briscoe presiding."

We rose. Judge Briscoe, a bespectacled old black man with short white hair, came in through the back door. He approached the bench and took his seat. So did the rest of us.

"Erie Township versus Kenneth Miller," Judge Briscoe said. "Defendant is charged with one count of arson and assault. How do you plead, Mr. Miller?"

"Not guilty," I said.

Judge Briscoe looked inquiringly at me. "No counsel?"

"I'm my own, your honor. I've seen a lot of *Matlock* reruns."

I heard laughter behind me, none from Jenny or Alex. They were a tougher audience.

"Proceed, Mr. Grady."

The prosecutor stood up. "Your Honor, I intend to prove that the accused did violently and without provocation assault the person of Ryder Coogan, a respected member of the community."

"Objection," I said.

"On what grounds?" asked Judge Briscoe.

"Misrepresentation. Ry Coogan—respected? He's a lying weasel, your honor."

There was voluminous laughter behind me. I thought I heard Alex join in, but not Jenny. Ry seethed. Judge Briscoe struck his gavel.

"Order. Objection, er, overruled."

Grady said, "The Prosecution calls Ken Miller to the stand."

I approached the witness stand and took the hot seat. Deputy Smith swore me in on a worn Bible. Grady neared me predatorily.

"Mr. Miller. Is it not true that on the evening of October eleventh, you attacked Ryder Coogan in his back yard, and consequently set fire to his home?"

"Objection," I said. "Counsel's badgering the witness."

"You can't object! You're the defendant!"

"And the defense," I said.

Judge Briscoe leaned over to Deputy Smith. "Get me two aspirin, will you, Gordy."

Deputy Smith went out through the judge's bench door.

"Objection overruled. Answer the question, Mr. Miller."

"He was going to shoot Jake," I said.

There was angry grumbling from the spectators, and loud hissing from Pedro and Tommy in the left aisle.

"Order!" said Judge Briscoe, pounding his gavel.

Deputy Smith reentered with a bottled water and two pills. He handed them to the judge, who took the pills and gulped the water.

"So," said Grady. "You attacked Mr. Coogan to stop him from shooting a dog on his own property. A dog that had just feasted on his prize chickens. A dog that had plagued Mr. Coogan for six months! Specifically, *that* dog!"

He whirled dramatically and pointed an accusatory finger at Jake in the row behind me. Everyone turned to the dog, including me. Jake whimpered. Jenny caressed his back.

"I couldn't let him shoot him," I said.

"Are you aware, Mr. Miller, of a law in this county that permits a person to shoot a dog, a cat, or any other animal on his own property?"

"I am. I read the bylaws of your town. It's dubbed the Old Yeller Law, and it applies strictly to the animal's owner. You can't just shoot any pet that drops by for tea, or moonshine."

I looked at Ry. Several others turned to him. Ry squirmed.

"I see," said Grady. "So if Mr. Coogan was in fact Jake's owner, he would then have the right to shoot him. In which case you'd be guilty of unprovoked assault, isn't that true?"

"Objection. Um—speculative?"

"Sustained."

I got one, I beamed.

"Your honor," said Grady, holding up the document he was reading earlier. "I have here a certificate of rabies' vaccination, dated almost two years ago, for a beagle of mixed breed name of Jake, and matching the description of that dog. In this whole county, no other dog matches this description."

Grady handed Judge Briscoe the paper. The judge perused it for a minute, then returned it to Grady. Grady approached me and handed me the document. I read it, feeling sicker by the line. My eyes fell on the first of two signatures.

"Who's Joshua McCrea?"

"He was vet here some thirty years," Judge Briscoe said fondly. "And one heck of a chess player. He passed away last year."

"Never mind the doctor's signature," said Grady. "Kindly read aloud the name of the dog owner."

"It's not true," I said, staring at the signature.

"Mr. Miller, please comply," said Judge Briscoe.

"Ry Coogan," I muttered.

"Louder please," said Grady.

"Ry Coogan."

There was grumbling from the spectator rows.

"Ry Coogan," said Grady. "That would explain, would it not, why the dog led you straight to Mr. Coogan's house. *His* house!"

"He was going to kill Jake," I said.

"As was and is his right under the Old Yeller Law, which you yourself have cited."

The grumbling in the courtroom got louder.

"He told me the dog wasn't his," I said. " 'That overgrown rat ain't mine,' he said."

"You must've misheard him, before you attacked him. I have no further questions."

Grady turned his back on me. The solemn spectators grumbled.

"Wait a minute!"

"You may leave the stand, Mr. Miller," said Judge Briscoe,

I stood up, and looked to where Jenny sat. She was gazing back at me with concern, probably for Jake. This would end worse for him than me. It gave me a desperate idea.

"The defense calls Jake the dog to the stand," I said.

The entire courtroom gasped.

"Objection," Grady said with a smirk. "This is a desperate theatrical ploy."

"Your honor," I said, "the prosecution has made Jake's ownership its main—nay, its only—argument as to my criminality in this case. I submit that ownership must be determined not by a suspicious document from a dead veterinarian, but by that special bond between man and dog."

Judge Briscoe appeared pensive for what seemed a while, then said, "I'll allow it. But don't test the court's patience, Mr. Miller."

I looked at Jake lying on Jenny's lap.

"Come on, Jake."

Jake looked up at the sound of his name. Other than that he didn't move.

"I'm trying to save your hide," I said. "And mine."

Jake didn't budge.

"Go on, boy," said Alex.

Jake moved left off of Jenny's lap, across Alex and Annie's, then jumped on the floor. He approached me with little interest. I tapped the witness chair.

"Jump."

Jake sprang up to the witness chair and sat down.

"What now, Mr. Miller?" said Judge Briscoe.

"With the Court's permission, I propose to let Jake choose between Ry Coogan and myself."

"What?!" decried Grady. "This is outrageous! It's a mockery of justice!"

Ry began persistently tapping Grady's back.

"The People won't stand for this, your honor! Excuse me."

Grady finally turned to Ry, who whispered something in his ear. The prosecutor nodded then addressed the bench.

"I withdraw my objection."

I disliked the sound of that. Judge Briscoe pensively stroked his chin, while the courtroom crowd chattered. The judge lowered his hand and looked at me.

"Mr. Miller, please stand by the right wall with your back to it."

I walked the ten paces to the right wall and turned, as if toward a firing squad.

"Mr. Coogan, kindly do the same by the left wall."

Ry moved to the center aisle then left. As he turned away from me, I saw the reason for his confidence. Four beef jerky sticks jutted out of his corduroy pants' back pocket. He reached the left wall and spun to face me.

"Gentlemen," said Judge Briscoe. "When I give the word, you'll both have one minute to call the dog to you. Gentle tones, no yelling. Stay within eight feet of your wall. If either one of you crosses over to the dog, I'll award custody of him to the other. Any questions?"

"Your honor," I said. "Coogan has beef jerky on him. Jake's kind of partial to that."

"I've got no legal reason to confiscate it. Do you wish to continue with this or not?"

"Yes, sir."

"Me too," said Ry.

Judge Briscoe studied his watch for about ten seconds then said, "Now."

"Jake," I said. "It's me, your old cellmate."

Jake glanced at me from the witness chair, then turned away. Ry whipped out two jerky sticks and brandished them at Jake.

"Here, boy! Nice, fresh beef! Your favorite!"

Jake hungrily eyed the jerky sticks. He jumped off the stand to the floor, facing Ry.

"Jake," I said. "Don't do it."

Ry bit into one of the meat sticks and chewed loudly. "Mmm mmm. Dee-licious. Come and get it!"

He waved the other stick at Jake. Jake took two cautious steps toward him. My chest tightened.

"Jake. Please stop."

Jake paused. He turned to me then looked away, and took two more steps toward Ry.

"That's it, boy," said Ry. "Come to papa."

Jake inched closer to Ry. I felt a lump in my throat, but spoke despite it.

"Jake. I'm sorry."

Jake halted, and looked back at me.

"I was a jerk."

Jake turned completely around to face me. Behind him, Ry grimaced.

"Stupid mutt, whatcha doin'?! Get your ass over here!"

There was loud grumbling in the courtroom.

"You're my best friend, Jake" I said. "The only real friend I've got. I'm sorry I let you down. You give me another shot at it, I won't let you down again."

Jake ran to me. He got up on his hind legs and started scratching my thighs with his front paws. I scooped him up to my face height. He eagerly licked my nose. I looked around the courtroom. Jenny and Alex were smiling, Jenny in tears, Alex with relief. Dunbar glared at Ry, and Ry at me. I barely heard Judge Briscoe.

"I find the defendant, Ken Miller, not guilty. And award him custody of Jake the dog. Case dis—"

"No!" Dunbar shouted. "You're through, Briscoe! You'll never judge in this town again!"

Jake growled at him in open hostility.

"Mayor Dunbar," said Judge Briscoe. "Shut the hell up."

Jake's growling loudened, as did Dunbar's voice.

"You're all a bunch of losers! Go ahead and vote for that fleabag! I'm sick of carrying your dead weight! And so's Max Shaw!"

"Max Shaw never heard of you!" Jenny said, rising to her feet. "Or El Dorado."

The courtroom went silent. I put Jake down on the floor, as curious as everyone else.

"Mrs. Garret, do you have something to add to these proceedings?" asked Judge Briscoe.

"My son does, your honor."

Judge Briscoe looked at Alex, sitting next to Jenny. "Approach the bench, young man."

Alex exited his row, holding the DVD case, and advanced to the bench. Every eye was on him, including mine. I saw the title on Alex's DVD case, *Empire*, Season 8.

"It's plain to see Jake doesn't like Mayor Dunbar," Alex said.

"The feeling's mutual," said Dunbar.

Jake growled as if on cue.

"Y'all hear that?" said Alex. "Something about the Mayor's voice rubs Jake wrong. Well, yesterday at the El Dorado site, I heard him react the same way, 'cept to Max Shaw's voice."

My brain pinged, though clearly slower than Alex's. "Despite the Australian accent," I said.

"I told my mom about that, and she remembered an episode of *Empire* she saw as a kid."

"Mom was a big fan," Jenny said.

"Beats all the junk on TV today," said Rose Perkins, sitting in the row behind her daughter, among the senior Jake Campaign workers.

"Lucky for us," Alex said, holding up the DVD, "Annie's dad has the whole series, including season eight. We watched that episode last night." He indicated the court clerk's laptop. "May I, Judge?"

"Leta, do you mind giving Mr. Garret your seat?" said Judge Briscoe.

The court clerk stood up. Alex sat down behind her large laptop. He inserted the DVD into a slot and tapped a few keys. Then he stood up and placed the laptop on Judge Briscoe's desk, screen facing the judge.

"Wait," said Judge Briscoe. "Let's share this with the court."

Alex spun the screen toward the rest of us. Judge Briscoe stood up and crossed the bar to my defender's table. He took a seat. I took the other. Jake jumped up on my lap like old times.

"Start the show, Mr. Garret," said Judge Briscoe.

Alex hit a laptop key.

On the screen appeared a luxurious swimming pool patio, behind a luxurious mansion. A superbly bodied blonde in a black bikini lay poolside on a recliner, sipping a martini. The mansion's door opened. Charles Dunbar, looking 20 years younger and dressed in buckskin, stepped outside. Blonde turned to him in surprise.

"Hi, darling. How'd you get here so fast? You called me from New York like two hours ago."

"I took a shooting star to get to you," Dunbar said in a thick Australian brogue.

On my lap, Jake growled.

"Why are you talking like that?" said Blonde.

"I hate to disappoint you, sheila, but I'm not Big John. I'm his cousin, Josh, from Australia. But we do share similar, ah, tastes."

Jake growled again.

"Why that's...!" Warren Boyle said.

"In what, for instance?" said Blonde.

"In beautiful women, for certain.

"Max Shaw's voice!" said Noah Richards.

"Yessir," said Alex, pausing the video. "And it didn't fool Jake. Not for one minute."

I said, "I've known two-faced politicians before, but never a two-voiced one."

The courtroom broke into excited chatter.

"This is better than *Matlock*," said Ruth Perkins.

Annie ran up through the bar gate to Alex, who warmly received her embrace. Judge Briscoe passed them on his return walk to the bench.

"It's a lie!" Dunbar said, stepping into the center aisle. "I'm not Shaw! I'm Charles Dunbar!"

A growling Jake leapt off his chair and charged Dunbar, chomping on his khaki leg. Dunbar pulled free of the dog, and rushed for the exit. Sheriff Harris stopped him in mid aisle, with a hand on his chest.

"Hold it, Mr. Mayor."

"How dare you!" said Dunbar.

"You're under investigation for fraud. You and Ry Coogan."

"All right," I said, raising my right fist.

"Your honor," Sheriff Harris said. "I request a warrant to search Mayor Dunbar's bank records. Reckon we'll find some local money raised for El Dorado in a secret account."

"Good plan, Dunbar," I said, almost sincerely.

"Oh, darling, is that true?" asked Lisa Dunbar in a quivering voice.

"You should know," said Dunbar. "You bought our house in Rio with it."

"Request granted," said Judge Briscoe.

I spotted Ry Coogan sneaking down the far left aisle toward the front. I ran down the center aisle and reached the door ahead of him, blocking his exit. Ry swung a wide right hook at me. I stopped it with my left wrist, and shot two right jabs to his jaw, followed by an uppercut. Ry went down for the count. I thought about kicking him in the ribs but decided I was better than him. Deputy Smith pulled Ry to his feet, and handcuffed him.

"That done it," said a red-haired farmer in the left back row. "I'm voting for Jake."

"Jake for Mayor!" shouted a young man behind the couple.

"Jake for Mayor!" yelled a woman near him.

Judge Briscoe pounded his gavel. "Order! Court hasn't been dismissed!"

I walked up the center aisle to approach the bar.

"I hate to break it to y'all," said Briscoe, "but a dog as mayor is out of the question. If there's presently no rule against it, there soon will be. Count on it."

There was a rumbling "Aww," from the spectators.

"You don't need Jake for Mayor," I said, turning to the stands.

Everyone looked at me, even Jenny.

"Jake's only a symbol, of your better angels. A reminder that you matter, all of you, just as you are—farmers, ranchers, merchants, teachers, parents. You are the foundation of this town. And that beats all the artificial riches Dunbar promised you.

'There's one among us who never forgot that. Whose faith in you never wavered. And who you'd be well served to have as your mayor. You all know who I mean. Jenny Garret."

"Whoa there, young fella," said a rugged-looking rancher standing near McKenna. "A girl Mayor? That's crazy talk."

I smiled. "Stranger things have happened."

Alex began to chant. "Jenny! Jenny! Jenny! Jenny!"

Annie joined her young man's refrain. "Jenny! Jenny! Jenny!"

Tommy and Pedro chimed in, "Jenny! Jenny! Jenny!"

More people took up the chant. "Jenny! Jenny!" Jenny!"

Jenny had a lump in her throat. She looked at me and shook her head, though with a winsome smile.

Judge Briscoe struck his gavel. "Case dismissed."

Sheriff Harris and Deputy Smith exited with their prisoners, Dunbar and Coogan. Nina and Bill followed, his video camera now handheld. The courtroom emptied as rapidly as it filled. Soon, just Jenny, Alex, Annie, and I remained, and Jake. Jenny regarded me as a medical student would a cadaver just before the dissection.

"Special Agent Garret," I said. "Brilliant work. You solved the case."

Alex grinned. Annie put her arm under his.

"Would you and Annie take Jake for a walk?" I said. "Though he's just another washed-up politician now."

Jake barked in protest.

"Come on, Jake," said Alex, and headed for the exit, arm in arm with Annie.

Jake looked from me to Jenny, then followed the young pair outside. I turned to Jenny, ready for her scalpel.

"That was quite a speech," she said.

"From the heart. Wasn't sure I had it in me."

"The speech or a heart?

I tapped my chest. "There's something beating fast in here, when you're around."

"Where's your honey?"

"It was spoiled. And sent back to Chicago."

"Reckon you'll be going there yourself now."

"Nope. Chicago's not my kind of town."

"What is?"

"Erie is."

Jenny smiled.

"Say, now that you're a politician, you've got to follow through on your promises."

"Such as?"

"More kisses where that one came from."

"Well," said Jenny, moving her lips toward mine, "I better get used to kissing babies."

And that she did, for a delightfully long time.

Epilogue

EYEWITNESS NEWS AUDIO FEED #72 (unedited)

Title: Mayor Jake Day
Location: Main Street, Erie, Colorado
Date/Time: Saturday, 12-9-2016, AM 10:31-11:02
Reporter: Nina Wallace

NINA: We're on Main Street in Erie, where what looks like the entire population is awaiting the appearance of one dog. The dog, Jake, was named Honorary Mayor of the town. Although a local judge, ah, curbed Jake's official race for Mayor, Erie residents decided to, well, throw him a bone...
CROWD CHEERS.
NINA: Here comes Jake, with his human entourage, to waves and cheers from the crowd. The four young people in front are Tommy Norton and Pedro Hernandez, followed by Annie Ross and Alex Garret. Alex is the son of Mayor-elect Jenny Garret, who last month handily beat incumbent mayor Charles Dunbar. Dunbar, a former TV star best known for the nineties' series *Empire*, is under house arrest, awaiting trial for fraud.

And here's Mayor-elect Garret herself, holding Jake's leash. Holding her other hand is Ken Miller, Jake's former Campaign Manager.

Ms. Garret, you'll be assuming office in two months. What will be your first act as Mayor?

JENNY GARRET: A sanctuary for abused and homeless animals, run by my new Director of Animal Welfare, Alex Garret, and his staff.

NINA: How exciting. Ken, as Jake's campaign manager, can you tell us what's in store for your dog in the future?

KEN MILLER: Well, Nina, the Colorado Senate race will be heating up next year. Jake just might be—

JENNY GARRET: Ken.

KEN MILLER: Er, fetching my slippers while I watch it on TV.

DOG BARKS.

JENNY GARRET: You sure you won't mind being my First Gentleman?

KEN MILLER: I'll be your only gentleman.

NINA: Someone once said, "Let sleeping dogs lie." That person never met Jake. In Erie, Colorado, this is Nina Wallace for *Headline News*.... Where to next, Bill?

BILL REYNOLDS (CAMERA MAN): Elvis sighting in Fort Collins.

NINA: Kill me now. What are you trying to say? Don't tell me my mike's still hot! Son of a—STATIC.

The End

About the Author

Lou Aguilar

Lou Aguilar is a fiction author and produced screenwriter.

Lou was born in Cuba, and lived there until age six, when his anti-Castro scholar father took the family to America one step ahead of the firing squad (for his dad, not Lou). He attended the University of Maryland, where he majored in English and minored in Film, and found both dependent on great writing. So Lou became, first, a journalist—a *Washington Post* and *USA Today* reporter—then a screenwriter, and now novelist.

Lou had three small movies produced, including the cult science-fiction film, ELECTRA (33 on *Maxim* magazine's list of "The 50 Coolest 'B' Films of All Time"). He presently writes only "A" scripts, and has a television legal drama and military thriller feature in development. Lou's last short story, "The Mirror Cracked", was published in *Kolchak: the Night Stalker Chronicles*

(http://www.iblist.com/book36867.htm), a prestigious horror anthology that was nominated for a Bram Stoker Award.

Lou is single, having postponed marriage until he either made the *New York Times* Best Sellers list or won an Oscar. That stipulation has become less rigid as the bird of youth tries to flutter away. *Jake for Mayor* is his first novel.

**If You Enjoyed This Book
Please write a review.
This is important to the author and helps to
get the word out to others
Visit**

PENMORE PRESS

www.penmorepress.com

All Penmore Press books are available directly through
our website, amazon.com, Barnes and Noble and Nook,
Sony Reader, Apple iTunes, Kobo books and via leading
bookshops across the United States, Canada, the UK,
Australia and Europe.

THE MAN IN THE SPIDER WEB COAT
BY
PHILIP ACKMAN

Titus Buchanan, a professor who runs a think tank at Williams College, believes he's figured out how to stage a successful revolution. When the United Nations adopts a historic vote spelling the end of colonialism, Buchanan seizes the opportunity to test his theory. His laboratory will be the Splendid Islands, a collection of palm-fringed cays scattered across three quarters of a million square miles of the South Pacific. Its inhabitants will be his lab rats.

But complications arise. The Splendids belong to New Zealand, and New Zealand has no intention of giving them up. The United States has its own secret "space age" agenda for the islands. The Queen of England is bound to support New Zealand, but she doesn't want Britain to fall out with the Americans, who favor independence. Meanwhile, the islanders, gripped with revolutionary fever, have ideas about self-rule. Reverend Geoffrey Brown, originally recruited by Buchanan to run the revolution, joins forces with an unlikely crew of locals and sets out to match wits with powerful opponents.

PENMORE PRESS
www.penmorepress.com

SAVED BY THE BANG

BY

MARINA J. NEARY

Welcome to 1980s Belarus, where Polish denim is the currency, "kike" is a pedestrian endearment, and a second-trimester abortion can be procured for a box of chocolates. Antonia Olenski, a catty half-Jewish professor at the Gomel Music Academy, wavers between her flamboyant composer husband, Joseph, and a chivalrous tenor, Nicholas. The Chernobyl disaster breaks up the love triangle, forcing Antonia into evacuation with her annoying eight-year-old daughter, Maryana.

After a summer of cruising through Crimean sanatoriums and provoking wounded Afghan veterans, Antonia starts pining for the intrigues and scandals of the Academy. When the queen of cats finally returns home, she finds that new artistic, ethnic, and sexual rivalries have emerged in the afterglow of nuclear fallout. How far will Antonia go to reclaim her throne?

PENMORE PRESS
www.penmorepress.com

Penmore Press

Challenging, Intriguing, Adventurous, Historical and Imaginative

www.penmorepress.com

CPSIA information can be obtained at www.ICGtesting.com
Printed in the USA
BVOW06s0412230716

456591BV00004B/5/P